Forgotten
in
Memory

Forgotten in Memory

Chloe Grant-Jones

The Book Guild Ltd

First published in Great Britain in 2017 by
The Book Guild Ltd
9 Priory Business Park
Wistow Road, Kibworth
Leicestershire, LE8 0RX
Freephone: 0800 999 2982
www.bookguild.co.uk
Email: info@bookguild.co.uk
Twitter: @bookguild

Typeset in Aldine401 BT

Printed and bound in the UK by TJ International, Padstow, Cornwall

ISBN 978 1911320 340

British Library Cataloguing in Publication Data.
A catalogue record for this book is available from the British Library.

For my Mother and Father –
I am a product of your strength and inspiration

And for Lauren Dawson –
For the conversation that changed the game

ONE

Joanna, Present Day

For the truly significant moments in life there are no impartial bystanders. There are no individuals uninvolved, unaffected, and free from being influenced by or influencing what they see. Instead there are witnesses and participants. Witnesses who, by the very definition of the word, see the actions of life taking place but do not directly involve themselves in what is taking place. They watch. They observe. They think. They observe the significant and the mundane. But who is to say which is which? Every day people go about their lives, noticing things that will soon be forgotten in memory, things their mind deems unworthy of their conscious being, things that nonetheless have altered the course of their mind from that point on. It is from the position of witness that we step forth as participants. We no longer exist as the secondary characters to another story, but instead we become the protagonists of our own.

But no matter what position you hold, you exist. You hold a place in the story. What role you have, what influence you hold, that is up to you.

Take the policeman for example. His name was Larry Royce. He was old; too old, his wife kept telling him. He had skin like crinkled paper, and fluffy grey hair that stuck up in tufts upon his head. He had to crouch down to look me in the eyes. It's fascinating what details stand out in our memories.

1

Screaming, crying, a blazing pain biting my left arm, and the policeman's fluffy grey hair.

I wonder what he remembers about me. I wonder if he can remember me at all, or if my part in his story has been lost in a chapter he can't recall. He delivered the news that changed my life beyond that which my ten-year-old mind could comprehend, and yet to him I simply could have been just another little girl orphaned during his shift. Aunt Katrina was inconsolable, and so it fell to him to explain to three children how something that had spared their lives had claimed that of their parents'. He was too old for this, his wife told him. He retired that year; I guess he finally believed her.

Screaming, crying, a blazing pain biting my left arm, and the policeman's fluffy grey hair.

'Joanna? Joanna!'

We were coming home from visiting the Taylors when it happened. They were family friends. Mrs Taylor always smelt like peppermint and Mr Taylor always positioned his glasses on the tip of his nose. We had been for dinner at their house. Mum had wanted to stay longer but Imogene had been in a foul mood so Dad said we had better be getting home. Jason and I weren't really bothered either way.

'Imogene, we will talk about this when we get home,' my Dad said, his voice firm but tired. Why did she always have to argue with him?

She continued arguing with him when we got in the car, and as he drove us down the dark country road. I had stayed quiet, with Jason on my left fiddling with the tie my mum had made him wear. My mum sat in the front seat, interjecting here and there, trying to calm them both down. Her long auburn hair flowed down her back so that some hung over the seat in front of me. She was so beautiful.

'Joanna, please! No… Joanna!'

I whispered for Imogene to let it go, but she didn't listen to me. She never listened to me. She was four years older, and dismissed me with a wave of her hand. It was a subtle motion indicating that I did not understand. I wanted to, but she would never tell me. Jason simply looked from Imogene, to Dad, to Mum, to me, and back again. He was four years old. They told Katrina his age protected him, that his innocence would cushion the pain that understanding wrought. I disagreed. He didn't understand, so all he could do was cry and tell us to bring them back.

Mum reached back behind her seat, her hand outstretched. I reached out mine and met my mother's hand. She squeezed my hand gently and turned to smile at me over the seat.

Then it hit us. Another car, bearing another driver, another life, and another story. The driver had lost control of his steering. The car hit us side on. I felt the glass as it sprayed my face. I clung to whatever my hands could grab. Like toys being thrown around in a child's bag it was as if we had no control over our own bodies.

My parents had felt little pain, they said. My parents had suffered little, they said.

I reached out my hand, seeking to meet the comfort of my mother's, but there's nothing there. This wasn't real.

'She's still unconscious. They've put her on something for the pain. I can't believe this is happening again.' It's funny how history can repeat itself.

Why didn't she listen to me all those years ago? If Imogene had just listened to me, if she had stopped arguing, then maybe

3

Dad would have paid more attention to the road. Maybe he would have seen the car coming. Maybe I should have spoken up. Maybe if I had done more to calm her down then we wouldn't have left the Taylors' house so early. Maybe then we would have missed the car.

But what about the other driver? I'm sure they asked themselves similar questions. After all, he played a part. After all, there are no bystanders. We became characters in his story and he in ours. Victims or villains, who's to say?

Screaming, crying, a blazing pain biting my left arm, a policeman's fluffy white hair and a mother's fading hand.

There are no bystanders; everybody plays a part.

TWO

Joanna, Three Months Earlier

'Imagine if a hooded man came up to you, handed you a giant leather-bound book and smiled, walking away without a single word. You begin to read it and you realise that this is a book of your entire life. From beginning to end, birth to death, every single event, every fear, every smile, moment of laughter and of love written down. What would you do? Would you read it to the end?'

I posed this question to my friends. We had all returned home from university and it was the first time we had seen each other since we had finished for summer. We were lying on blankets in my garden, soaking up the first rays of the summer sun.

'I don't know,' Simon replied, 'it would suck if your life didn't turn out how you wanted it to and there was nothing you could do about it but roll with the punches.'

'Then again, if you knew that something truly awful was going to happen then you could change it, stop the bad stuff from happening before it actually happened. Rewrite the plot,' Leo said, choosing to see the more optimistic side to it.

Simon and Leo looked fairly similar; they were both tall, with light brown hair, a fairly muscular build, and had often been mistaken for brothers. But where Simon's hair sat in smooth waves upon his head, Leo's flowed in unruly curls.

Leo's crooked smile made it look as if he was always laughing at something, but Simon's was softer and less frequently seen, so that when you did see him smile you knew he meant it.

'What kind of question is that?' Charlie asked haughtily as she lounged back on the recliner. 'Sounds like something my weird aunt would ask me.'

'Well I think Meredith and I would get on very well in that case,' I laughed. 'I didn't come up with it. Mrs Vincent asked me a couple days ago,' I shrugged.

Charlie just snickered.

'I like Mrs Vincent,' Abbey said sincerely. 'She always smiles at me when I pass by and asks how I am. But not in the typical "I'm just being neighbourly" way, but in a way where she genuinely sounds interested.'

Mrs Vincent was an elderly woman who lived next door to us. She was short and stout with long, dark grey hair that she always wore in a French braid. I had known her since we moved to the house when I was little and she had always been kind to us. Her age had left her slightly hunched and her skin wore the trials of her long life, but she wasn't fragile. That's what I liked most about her; she wasn't what you expected her to be.

'Maybe the four of you could form a club,' Charlie jested, playing with a lock of Abbey's hair. Charlie's long black hair flowed in curls around her face, accentuating her pale porcelain skin, and sea-green eyes.

'Shall we get jackets?' I joked to Abbey, and Charlie rolled her eyes playfully. 'Anyway, you didn't answer my question. Would you read the book?'

'Oh I don't know,' Charlie sighed boredly, 'Why not? Might be kind of fun knowing everything that is going to happen to everyone else in your life before they do.'

'But it would change how you look at everyone. You wouldn't be able to interact the same way with anyone once you knew. No, I wouldn't like it. I wouldn't want to know how everyone's stories end, least of all mine!' Abbey shivered at the thought.

'I agree with Abbey,' Leo nodded in agreement. 'It's like knowing the plot of a film before you actually watch it; it takes all the fun out of the thing.'

'What about you, Simon?' I asked, shadowing my eyes against the glare of the sun so that I could look at him properly.

'It depends. Can you change things once you've read the book? Alter the course of things if you didn't like how it turned out?'

'I guess so,' I pondered aloud. 'I think it would be hard to resist trying to change things.' I brushed the scars on my arm mindlessly as I spoke. I looked up and Simon was frowning at me. He wasn't doing it obviously, but I had learnt to read his face over the years. I looked away from his gaze and smiled nonchalantly. 'Even if I couldn't, though, even if there was some rule that you weren't allowed to change anything once you read the book, I think I would still read it. Just out of curiosity.'

'Curiosity killed the cat,' Charlie added mockingly.

'But satisfaction brings it back,' Leo retorted.

At that point we heard the front door open and then slam to a close with a definitive crash.

'Maybe we should ask Imogene what she thinks,' Simon asked, his droll tone suggesting we should do anything but that.

'She would probably just steal the book from the poor mysterious man, and then use it to take over the world, burning and pillaging as she went.'

'Thank you, Leo, for that brilliant description,' Charlie said wryly. 'You can go ask her and we'll make sure your funeral is just how you would have liked it.'

'Guys, stop,' Abbey said apologetically. She was always

more tactful about her dislike of my sister than the others. It wasn't really in her nature to dislike anybody. 'Charlie, we should probably get going anyway, our shift starts soon.'

Charlie sighed dramatically before grunting in assent. She and Abbey had started summer jobs waitressing at Abbey's parents' restaurant. Neither of them enjoyed it but both were too broke to indulge their contempt for waiting tables.

'Oh, can you guys give me a lift home? I have some reading I need to start,' Leo said, lumbering up from where he had been lying down, gathering his stuff together.

'Take a break for once, Leo,' Charlie laughed, tying her hair back into a loose pony-tail. 'You've been home for like two weeks. Your summer has only just begun!'

'I know, which means I have exactly three months until I get back to uni. Which in turn means I have exactly three months to read a ton of stuff, write a few essays and plan my great escape from the clutches of my Cambridge professors,' Robby sighed, shaking his head in mock despair.

I laughed, patting him on the shoulder, and he threw his arms around me pulling me into a rough bear hug. I said goodbye to the others and heard the front door close behind them as I bent down to collect up the blankets off of the grass.

'You've got to give him credit,' Simon said, as he helped me tidy up the garden.

'Why's that?'

'Well, for starters, none of us actually thought he would get in.'

It was true. Leo possessed absolutely zero common sense. For example, on his way to a university interview he had once spent three and a half hours on a train before realising that it was going in the wrong direction. Like I said, he had no common sense and yet he had been top of our year in every subject he had chosen to study at A-level. He had then been one of only three people from our school to get into Cambridge last year.

He was studying Natural Sciences. Like most of us he had no idea what he wanted to do after university, but that was a conversation we had made a conscious effort to avoid, myself most of all.

All five of us had decided to go to university last September. We had all known it was the step we wanted to take, or rather the step we had to take; we just didn't know what it was a step towards. Katrina told me that we would all know in time.

'If only that book thing was true. Then we'd be sorted,' Simon grumbled as we moved the blankets inside the house.

'I don't know what you're complaining about. You have a better idea than any of us.'

'Studying Law doesn't necessarily mean you want to be a lawyer,' he shrugged. 'It's just a stepping stone. For all you know I could be President.'

'Maybe you should move to a country where they actually have a president,' I said patronisingly.

'Well, we can rule out comedian as your future career.'

'Oh, I don't know about that. I always thought you were pretty funny,' my Aunt Katrina said, bustling into the kitchen. She put shopping bags on the counter at which Simon and I sat.

'Hey! I didn't hear you guys come in.'

My brother Jason was walking behind her, his nose buried in a book.

'Jason, put that book down and help with the shopping, please.' Katrina kissed me on the head and said hello to Simon. 'How's your mum, Simon?'

'She's good thanks, just busy,' he replied, helping himself to some food from the bags in front of him.

'Well, I'm sure she's very happy to have you home for a couple months.'

He just smiled in response. Simon's mum worked a lot.

She was a single mum so she always had a lot on her plate. I think it strained Simon more then he let on. He wasn't the type to complain.

'How's your book?' I asked Jason, turning around on my stool.

'I'm so nearly finished. Which is good because Simon has given me another one to read that he says is even better,' Jason replied without lifting his eyes from the page.

'It's true,' Simon said, in between eating some grapes he had stolen from a bag on the counter. '*Flood Child* was a favourite of mine when I was your age. I've got a couple more I want to give you as well when you're done with that one.'

Jason looked up at him excitedly and Simon grinned down at him. Simon didn't have any siblings and Jason didn't have any brothers, so the two of them had adopted each other to make up for it.

'Wait, weren't you meant to be staying over at Ben's tonight? I thought you were going to take him after work?' I asked, looking from Jason to Katrina.

Simultaneously they both looked up at me and then at each other, as I raised my eyebrows at them. Simon burst out laughing as Katrina darted to her bag, grabbed her car keys, and the two of them ran up and down the stairs getting Jason's bag together. They yelled their goodbyes as they left through the front door. But then two seconds later Jason ran back into the kitchen to pick his book up from where he had left it on the kitchen table.

'Bye, Simon!'

'Have fun!' Simon yelled back, still laughing.

'Bye to you too,' I shouted after him sarcastically.

We heard Katrina's car as it drove away. The sound of Katrina bustling about the kitchen was replaced by the gentle melancholic tones of Imogene's cello music streaming down the stairs. I laid my left arm in my lap and traced the pale lines of my scars gently with the fingertips of my right hand. I had started doing it without even thinking.

'Are you going to talk to her about it?' Simon asked. I looked up and he was watching me with the same look he had had in the garden, his dark green eyes boring into my hazel.

'What are you doing for dinner? Katrina was talking about ordering pizza tonight,' I said, getting up to finish unpacking the bags of shopping that had been left discarded about the kitchen.

'Joanna...'

'Or we could just cook something here? Oh, she bought stir-fry. We could just have that?'

'Joanna,' he repeated. 'You said you wanted to talk to her. What's stopping you?'

I paused where I stood, my hand on a cupboard handle, my back to him. I sighed but didn't turn around. 'I changed my mind.'

'The anniversary is three months away, Jo.' His voice was firm and knowing, but not unkind. He was never unkind, but his tone wasn't what I had an issue with. He had got up from his chair and stood behind me, leaning on the side of the kitchen island. I let my raised arm fall to my side as another sigh escaped me. 'I'm sorry. I don't want to push you, I just want this year to be different. You know what I mean.'

I turned around slowly and let my posture relax as I slumped against the counter-top. I met his gaze. He looked so much older, as if he had aged ten years in the ten months he had been away at university. His jaw seemed more pronounced and he had let his hair grow out longer.

I smiled gently at him, as he stood there frowning under the weight of my problems. 'I know you do. I'll talk to her,' I said, hoping my smile wasn't as strained as my voice. He smiled back, but it didn't quite reach his eyes. The sound of her cello still floated down the stairs, encompassing us in its melodic grips. 'Now, what shall we eat?' I asked, allowing my voice to regain the lightness it had possessed mere moments ago.

Katrina arrived home half an hour later, her reddish hair slightly more dishevelled than usual. Simon stayed for dinner and then I offered to drive him home. I know he probably could have just walked home but it had gotten really late and I like driving at night. Listening to music under the urban stars that were street lights, with the speed of driving: What's not to love? I took the longer route to Simon's house by his request as he was having too much fun singing along to the radio. By the time we got to his house my cheeks were sore from laughing too much, and Simon had started to go hoarse from singing.

I pulled up to his house, but before he got out of the car he paused. He smiled and said goodnight, but he lingered.

'You're doing better than you think. I hope you know that.'

All I could do was smile back. He got out of the car and I drove home with the radio still on. I was no longer listening to the music and I was no longer singing along, but I didn't want it to be silent. As I drove home I sped up, I drove faster than I should. I just didn't want my mind to wander.

'You're doing better than you think': What does that mean?

In three months I would be acknowledging the anniversary of my parent's death. Simon was wrong. I wasn't doing better than I thought, because I had no idea how I was meant to be feeling.

When I got home Katrina had gone to bed. I made sure the house was locked up but as I was walking across the second floor landing I noticed Imogene's light was still on. I knocked lightly on her door and pushed it open.

'Can we talk?'

THREE

Imogene

I looked up. Joanna stood holding her left arm in her right, leaning on my door-frame. Her auburn hair hung to directly below her chin. She pushed a lock of hair behind her ear as she stood, fidgeting.

'What do you want?' I asked, looking back down at my notebook. I was sitting on my window-chair with my notebook laid open on my lap, a pencil dancing between my fingertips. It was a cloudless night and so I had a direct view of the ocean from my window.

She didn't answer but stood awkwardly, brushing her right hand up and down her left arm. She was always doing that. 'I have work to do, Joanna, so what do you want?' I sighed brusquely. It wasn't exactly true; I hadn't written any new music for months, but I had chosen to lie rather than feign patience.

'What are you working on?' she asked, stepping into my room and leaning forward on my bed frame.

I closed my notebook and shoved it aside. 'It's late, Joanna, so if you don't actually have anything to say, close the door on your way out.'

'I did… I mean I do,' she stuttered. 'Have you spoken to Katrina?'

'Oh, for goodness sake, Joanna,' I said, already irritated.

I leant back against the wall where I sat and looked up at her bitterly.

'It's not unreasonable, Imogene. We just want to make sure you'll be there—'

'No,' I interjected, a smile playing on the corners of my lips, 'you want to make sure I don't make a scene.'

'Because that's so beyond imagination,' she grumbled, her voice dripping with sarcasm. I clamped my lips together, and shook my head, glaring out of the window. She sighed. 'It's been nine years, Imogene,' she said, as if that detail would have slipped my mind. She made me feel like a child. She was only ten years old when it happened, and as she stood there, chewing the inside of her lip, rolling back and forth on the balls of her feet, she still looked like a child.

'I've already told Katrina I can't go.' I spoke bluntly, rising from the window seat, gathering my sheet music together.

'You can't go? What do you mean you can't go?' she asked, her tone incredulous.

'I have other plans.'

She laughed humourlessly. 'You're ridiculous.'

I turned to look at her, equally sombre. 'I don't think I'm the one being ridiculous here.'

'I'm ridiculous for expecting you to be with your family on the anniversary of your parents' *death*?'

'You're ridiculous if you think that this little thing you do every year actually has any point to it. You're ridiculous if you think a bonfire and a dinner on the anniversary of Benson and Vera's death is going to make a scrap of difference.' Without realising I had crossed the room and was standing directly in front of her. I lowered the volume of my voice, but my enmity was not hidden. 'And you're ridiculous if you haven't realised how truly *pathetic* you're being.' I took a step back and sighed. 'Like I said, I have other plans. You need to grow up, Joanna, and you can't do that by staying lost in the past.'

Her lip was trembling and tears escaped the corners of her eyes before she could brush them brusquely away. 'I hate you,' she whispered.

I clenched my teeth. Tears would not escape *my* eyes.

Shaking her head she turned and walked away, her fists clenched by her sides. But before she left she paused, holding the door handle tightly. She kept her back to me, only inclining her head slightly in my direction as she spoke. 'When did you start doing that?'

'Doing what?' the exasperation clear in my voice.

She turned around to look me in the eyes. 'When did you stop calling them Mum and Dad?'

I didn't answer but turned back towards the window. The moonlight was bouncing off my pale blue wallpaper. It made my room look like a reflection of the ocean it was looking out on, with the only other light being a lamp standing next to Joanna. The lamplight accentuated the golden tones of her hair and brought warmth to her pale complexion. As I turned from the warm glow of the lamp to the blanched tones of the moon I crossed my arms tightly across my chest. She couldn't make me explain. I heard the door close quietly behind me.

When I realised they weren't really mine, I thought to myself.

I crossed the room to where my gold-framed mirror hung above my chest of drawers. I looked at myself, illuminated in the lamplight. My blonde hair had grown lighter in the summer sun. I wore it long, with my curls flowing almost to my hips. The curls were unruly, flowing erratically and asymmetrically. My skin had gained a golden tone to it so that my blue eyes pierced my reflection. I looked nothing like them. Joanna looked so much like her, but I didn't look like any of them. Jason and Joanna both had Vera's auburn hair and Benson's hazel eyes. I looked like no one but myself, and as I gazed into the mirror I did not even recognise her. She looked so broken. There just weren't enough pieces left to put together a smile. My vision blurred. I wiped away the tears angrily and banged my fists on the chest of drawers.

I didn't look like any of them.

I was a small child when Vera and Benson brought me home with them. I didn't know my biological parents. I didn't want to know them. Sometimes I think I remember them, but I know it's only my mind playing tricks on me, the fallout from the battle between a child's imagination and memory.

As I turned off the lamplight and climbed under my duvet I remembered a time when I wasn't this angry. But these days when the memories flowed so did the tears.

I dreamed of them.

I was running. I was running so fast. I screamed for them. I screamed until my lungs burned, but I screamed through the flames. I was down on the beach. I could hear my cello playing softly. I screamed for them but they wouldn't answer. Why didn't any of them answer?

One set of parents replaced by another, and yet two sets of parents out of the reach of my grasping hands. But I kept running.

I woke up with a thin layer of sweat covering my entire body, my hair clinging to the top of my head. The morning sun streaming through my window had woken me up. I had forgotten to shut my curtains. The ocean glistened in the distance, an image of peaceful perfection. I remained in bed for a bit longer, trying to piece together the scenes I had dreamed.

Joanna didn't understand. How could she? She was a baby when I joined the family. We had been happy. I would be a liar to say we hadn't been happy. But as I got older I just found it harder. I found it harder to let things go. I didn't look anything like them. Then the accident happened, and they became another memory. Another image I would run towards in my dreams, unable to hold within my grasp. Nine years on, and it wasn't any easier; I wasn't any happier.

Joanna didn't understand. I didn't expect her to.

I climbed out of my bed, tying my hair back into a loose bun. I got changed into a pair of ripped jeans and a loose T-shirt. I walked slowly to the bathroom and took my time getting ready. I could hear music playing downstairs, and as I walked into the kitchen I was greeted by Katrina eating breakfast at the kitchen table with the radio blaring.

'Good morning, sunshine,' she said sarcastically with her mouth full of cereal.

'Morning,' I mumbled back, turning the radio down before making myself breakfast.

As I sat down opposite her she was eyeing me, smiling. She was the type of person who smiled at everything.

'What are you looking at me like that for?'

'Joanna told me about your pleasant little conversation last night,' she said, scooping more cereal into her mouth. I rolled my eyes as she raised her eyebrows at me. 'I know it might be pushing it, seeing as you're already so delightful, but maybe try to be a bit kinder to her over the next couple of weeks. Maybe… oh, I don't know, try not stamping on whatever happiness she gains from trying to remember your parents,' she said. Her voice was sarcastic and light-hearted, but her expression told me she wasn't joking.

'I've already told you I'm not going.'

'And I'm telling you to rethink that. This is important to her, Imogene, and once a year, just *once*, I expect you to make the effort.' She sighed and resumed eating her cereal. 'Then every other day of the year you can go back to being your typical, charming self,' she laughed.

'You're hilarious,' I told her wryly. 'Is she up yet?'

'Yeah, she's gone for a run.'

17

I stood up finishing my cereal quickly. 'I'm going to be late,' I said placing my bowl in the sink and shoving the cereal box back into the cupboard.

'Late to where?'

'I'm meeting Mary and Theo.'

'Who's Theo? What kind of name is *Theo*?'

I couldn't help but smile as I kissed her goodbye on the cheek. 'I kinda like it.'

I paused by the door, turning back to face her. 'Oh, how did your interview go?'

She shook her head and smiled up at me sadly. 'Something will come along soon. But never mind that, *Theo* awaits you,' and she waved me away dramatically.

Katrina had a degree in Art History and had been working as a teaching assistant. She loved working with children but it wasn't what she wanted to be doing. She had been interviewing at different art galleries in town, but had so far been unlucky. However, she kept trying and would approach each interview with the hearty optimism that she and Joanna seemed to hold in abundance.

As I was leaving the house I heard Katrina greet Joanna as she came in the back door from the beach path. I left through the front door, closing it quietly behind me. As I walked into town I pondered what Katrina had told me. I didn't mean to be so harsh to Joanna, but she had a very different way of seeing things to me; and in our case, where there was difference, there was inescapable conflict. I put my earphones in and blared my thoughts away.

I arrived at the coffee shop after Mary and Theo. They were deep in conversation when I joined them.

I had been at university with Mary. She was shorter than I was, so that she seemed to disappear into the chair she sat on. She had recently cropped her hair into a pixie cut, so that her jet black hair stuck out on her head. She matched her new hair cut with blood-red lipstick that suited her olive skin tone nicely. After university we had both gone on to get jobs at a local recording studio, but whilst I got offered a part-time position as I wasn't sure I wanted to commit, Mary had begun working there full-time and had thrived in her position. When I sat down she was busy telling Theo about a recent project she had been working on.

Theo sat in the other armchair opposite me, humouring Mary as she rattled on. He winked at me when I sat down. I had met Theo when I started playing for the city orchestra. He was tall with blond hair that he never styled, and a tattoo that peeked out of his long-sleeved shirt.

I breathed out as I sat down and waited for Mary to finish her story. They were my haven. However, sometimes, the closer you are with someone, the more entitled they feel to hold an opinion on your life.

I told them about my conversation with Joanna.

'Wow. I would have slapped you if you were my sister,' Mary said, sipping her cappuccino.

'Thanks,' I said sarcastically, but I couldn't stop the heat from rushing to my cheeks.

'Why don't you just go? It's just one night,' she shrugged.

'I'm not going because I don't want to. It's as simple as that,' I said, my tone biting but my voice quiet.

'People deal with things in different ways. Why should she have to do something she doesn't want to?' Theo spoke up, leaning back in his chair. 'Anyway, we have plans that night.'

'She can go to a party any night of the year, next week for example,' Mary laughed incredulously, looking back and forth from Theo to me. 'Just think about it, hun. Your aunt makes a lot of sense. If it's important to your sister to remember your parents in this way…'

'They weren't even Imogene's parents!' Theo laughed

19

facetiously, his dark eyes hardening. Mary looked at him, stunned.

'What's your point?' I asked bitterly, through clenched teeth.

'Look, I didn't mean to be so blunt,' he said apologetically, his lips curled up at the sides, 'I just meant, you don't owe them anything.'

'They were still her parents,' Mary said quietly, her voice defensive. She had never been a fan of Theo's bluntness. I had never minded so much. I usually admired his honesty, but now I just wasn't in the mood.

I avoided looking at them both. Eventually they moved on to a new topic and I joined in here and there, but I wasn't paying attention. I looked around the coffee shop instead. It was filled with people in suits getting their morning caffeine fix, and groups of young teenagers with nowhere better to be, and the odd individual lost to the world by the transfixion of their phone.

Over on the window seat I noticed a couple of Joanna's friends. It was that annoying girl Charlie who was always flirting with every guy that came her way, and Simon. I didn't even know they were that close. They had both been friends with Joanna for years. We had known Simon and his mum ever since I could remember. I had always got the impression that those two were only friends because of the mutuality of Joanna's friendship. But as I looked over to them, Charlie put her hand on Simon's arm caressingly, leaning closer to him. Simon had always been hard to read, so I read all I could from the situation from the blatant obviousness of Charlie's body language.

'Huh,' I said, narrowing my eyes.

Theo and Mary looked up and gazed across to where I was looking. Theo looked back at me quickly. 'Do you know him?'

'Friends of my sister,' I shrugged, taking a sip from my

mug. At that point Simon looked up at me and met my stare. He pulled his arm from Charlie's and his posture became rigid. I laughed into my mug. So much for him being hard to read.

'Are we still on for next week?' Mary asked me.

'Of course,' I smiled at her.

When I looked back over to the window seat, Charlie and Simon were gone.

FOUR

Simon

As I strode down the street the summer sun streamed through the canopy of the trees that lined the road. I turned down a side road and the noise of the main roads was left behind me. I caught a glimpse of my reflection in a parked car and realised how deeply I was frowning.

Charlie had texted me earlier in the morning, asking me to meet her. I didn't often meet up with her alone. I wouldn't have thought anything of it, if it had been any of the others, but Charlie and I really hadn't spoken much outside of the group since we left for university.

She had broken up with her most recent boyfriend a couple of weeks ago, and from what Joanna had told me she hadn't coped very well with the split. She probably just wanted a friend, I had thought, and the others were probably busy.

In the coffee shop we just chatted for a bit. I listened and waited for her to come to the point, but she didn't. She just kept talking. Imogene put me on edge. I didn't like the way she looked at us.

I will call Joanna as soon as I get home, I thought. *Just to check in.*

As I rounded another corner a little boy about Jason's age sped past me on a bike. Two other boys followed and yelled their greetings at me excitedly. They were boys from my road. I turned in a circle as I called back to them, laughing.

'Good morning, Simon.'

When I turned back around Mrs Vincent was standing in front of me, as the bus she had just got off drove down the road behind her. She was wearing loose, light-green trousers and a pale purple top, with her long braid hanging over her left shoulder as usual.

'How are you?' I asked politely, walking towards her.

'Oh, I can't complain. Lovely day isn't it,' she mused, looking up towards the blue sky and then back at me. 'I'm actually on my way to see your mum. Walk with me?'

I nodded and smiled as we proceeded slowly down the road.

'How's Robert?'

'He has his good days, and he has his bad. But he's still my Robert,' she smiled nostalgically, looking forward down the pavement.

There was a light breeze and I lifted my head up and breathed out in unison with it. The wind made the leaves dance above us and created shadows that flickered across the objects below. I looked down at my hand as the shadows danced across it. I didn't really know what to say.

My mum had told me about Mrs Vincent's husband. He had been diagnosed with dementia a couple of years ago. As I looked over at her, smiling up into the sun, I realised that if I were to pass by her on this path, a simple bystander, I would not have known this thing that had taken hold of her life. You never know the stories people are hiding away in the libraries of their hearts.

'Is he still enjoying his books?' I asked, brushing my hair back against the wind.

She laughed lightly to herself. 'Every day he'll sit up in his library. "The smell of the ocean, my wife and my books, that's all I need", that's what he'll say to me. I was never much of a reader myself. Could never concentrate as long as him,' she chuckled. 'Now, Joanna, on the other hand, she and Robert could talk for days about those books of his.'

'That doesn't surprise me,' I smiled.

'How is she? I haven't spoken to her for a few days,' she asked earnestly. I looked over and she was waiting for my response with clear concern.

'She's OK.'

'Now, Simon, if I wanted a polite but fruitless answer like that I would have asked the postman how she was. You're a good boy, Simon, but I'm going to ask you again. How is she?' Her face was unreadable as she repeated herself.

I sighed. 'I don't know. I think she's struggling a bit being home from uni. This time of year will never be easy for her, and I don't think she would ever admit it, but I think she liked the distance of being away at university.'

I picked a leaf off a bush as we passed, and picked at it with my fingers. We were nearly at my house and I could see our car parked outside, down the road.

'Ah. And how's that sister of hers?'

I grunted. 'She makes life hard for Joanna. Harder than it needs to be.'

Mrs Vincent nodded her head solemnly. 'She's fighting a whole other battle, that girl.'

I didn't answer immediately, but looked away to the other side of the road. 'She took off last year without telling any of them where she was going, and then turned up wasted three days later.' I threw the leaf I had been picking at into the wind. 'The year before that she threw a drink at their family photos and claimed her glass slipped out of her hand,' I added, my voice growing increasingly bitter.

We had arrived outside my house. I opened the gate for her. She paused inside the gate and looked up at me. She was frowning against the sun and her eyes glinted harshly in the light. But her expression was pensive as she held my gaze.

'Imogene's slipped up, Simon. She has made mistakes and she will bear the consequences of those mistakes in full. But we must remember that she is also still hurting. We all bear our armour differently when life throws spears our way.' She sighed, and as she tucked a loose bit of grey hair behind her ear, I noticed how deeply the lines marked her face and how thin her hair had grown. She looked back up at me and smiled amiably, the creases around her eyes deepening. 'You've been a good friend to Joanna, but don't let that stop you from being a friend to others who may need one.'

At that point we heard the front door open and my mum stood at the top of the path, still in her work clothes. 'Are you two going to stand out there all day?' she called.

Mrs Vincent didn't stay for long. My mum offered her tea and cakes, and they chatted about the summer bustle. Mum complained about still having to work so much and Mrs Vincent listened kindly. After a while, Mrs Vincent excused herself and said she had better be getting back to Robert. I had always found their friendship entertaining. They couldn't be further apart in occupation and they were hardly similar in age, yet they got on like ocean waves and beach sand.

I spent the rest of the day at home, laid back in the garden with earphones in. Mum had to go back to work shortly after Mrs Vincent left. I think she felt guilty about working so much when I was home for the summer. She would never say it, but she always lingered indecisively before she walked out of the door. Then, when she was talking to Mrs Vincent, she kept peering over at me when she complained about work. It had bothered me a bit when I was younger, but as I had grown up the realities had sunk in. If anything, I felt guilty that she had to work so hard.

As I lay back on a sun lounger with my arm behind my head, I let my thoughts drift into careless wandering. I thought about my mum, I thought about how much I missed uni, I thought about the future, and I thought about the past. I thought about Mrs Vincent, and then unsurprisingly I thought about Joanna. I thought about what people do in an effort to be a friend to someone.

Humans are overcome by emotions that drive us to protect one and other, to care for that person and to see that their lives are happy, in whatever way we define that word to be. But what about those associated to our friends? Those people in their lives but not so much in ours? I cared about Joanna, and I cared about Jason. I liked Katrina, and I had liked Vera and Benson. But every feeling and thought I had ever entertained about Imogene had originated in relation to my feelings for the others. I disliked her because of how she treated her family. But as I laid there, my mind swirling with previously un-pondered thoughts, I realised I had never even considered trying to be a friend to Imogene.

An image flashed across my mind of the guy she was with in the coffee shop that morning. He was tall with bronze coloured hair. I hadn't paid much attention to him but he had worn a smirk that made him look as if the world were a joke that only he knew the punch line to. From what I could remember Joanna telling me, I thought he was one of the guys Imogene had disappeared with last year.

I was still thinking about this when I was walking through town the next day. I had got a job doing admin work at one of the solicitors' offices in town. It was only a couple of days a week, and I knew that even if I didn't know what exactly I wanted to do after uni, I just had to do something this summer to keep my mum satisfied.

It was my break, and I was standing in the queue at a coffee shop to buy my lunch when I noticed Imogene sitting alone at one of the corner tables. She had her earphones in and was bent over some papers. She didn't see me coming when I walked over to her.

She looked up at me when I was standing directly in front of her.

'What do you want?' she asked disinterestedly, pulling her earphones out.

'I'm good, thanks for asking. But enough about me, how are you?' I asked, heavily sarcastic.

She stared at me. 'Nope, it's definitely not your sophisticated wit that Joanna sees in you. So what exactly is it that makes my sister tolerate you?' She tapped her chin with her finger, mockingly.

'Oh, I don't know. Maybe not turning up to family memorials drunk as a skunk is a point in my favour.' Her face fell and turned cold as ice.

This was not going how I had planned.

'Well, as much as I love these little chats of ours, I'll have to take a rain-check,' she said, belligerently gathering up her things.

'Imogene,' I sighed, brushing my hair back. 'Can you just listen for two seconds?'

She stopped gathering her things and looked up at me curiously.

'I'm listening.' She raised her eyebrows at me impatiently.

I swallowed before trying again to be civil. 'I know we've never exactly seen eye to eye.' She guffawed. 'But...' I paused, trying to word it in the most amicable way possible, 'your family means a lot to me. And I know from how we talk to each other that you would have had to be a genius to figure it out, but that includes you.'

'OK,' she interrupted me, pushing her seat aside as she stood up and began shoving her things roughly into her bag. Out of the corner of my eye I noticed something flutter to the floor from her pile. 'I don't know what all this is about. Maybe you've been reading too many Nicholas Sparks books, I don't know. But let me make myself perfectly clear.'

She stood in front of me, and as she was equal in height to myself, her intense blue eyes bore evenly into mine. But her voice wasn't as harsh as I had been expecting; where I had been expecting venom, I received concern.

'My family is none of your business. I know just how much you care about my sister, Simon. But that's just it. Where my relationship with my sister is concerned, you have no opinion. Stay out of it.'

I didn't say anything in response. She sighed, looked down at the table beside us, brushed her hair brusquely behind her ear and walked past me to the door.

Well, that went well, I thought. Something made me think that wasn't what Mrs Vincent had in mind when she told me to try to be her friend.

As I was walking out of the shop door onto the bustling street pavement I heard someone calling behind me.

'Excuse me!' A woman wearing an apron came running out of the shop after me. 'Sorry, I think you dropped this. It was under the table you were at.' She handed me a folded piece of paper.

'Oh. Thanks.' I took it, and she smiled and went back into the shop. It was the piece of paper I had seen fall to the floor from Imogene's bundle. Although I didn't fancy another confrontation, I looked down the road to see if she was still around. I couldn't see her. I frowned as I looked down at the paper in my hand.

I unfolded the piece of paper to see if it was something I could just throw away and forget about: It definitely wasn't.

'Perfect,' I mumbled to myself.

I spent the rest of the day at work trying my hardest to concentrate, but failing miserably. I caught the bus to Joanna's house after work, rather than walking. It was too hot and I couldn't be bothered, even though I had walked to and from work every other day.

When I arrived at their house, Joanna was on the front step with a book on her lap.

'Hey!' she called to me as I walked up the path, smiling broadly. She closed one eye and held up her hand against the glare of the sun. 'I didn't know you were coming. How was work?'

'Who would have known that doing filing for minimum wage would be so mind-numbing,' I joked, setting myself down on the step next to her.

She laughed gently. 'Just wait until you get to do it nine to five every day for the rest of your life,' she replied flippantly. 'Shall we go in? I'm hungry.'

'Yeah. I'm just going to use your bathroom first.'

As I walked up the stairs I could hear music drifting out from a bedroom down the hall. The soft melancholic tones of a cello echoed down the stairs, greeting me as I walked onto the landing.

I knocked quietly on the door, and pushed it open. Imogene was sitting on her desk chair with her cello between her legs. She tilted her head to the side and let her bow fall as I walked in.

'I'm not sure how you think that conversation went, Simon, but for me it definitely didn't leave me yearning for another one.'

'You dropped this at the cafe,' I said, handing her the paper. I stepped back and put my hands in my pockets. 'One of the waitresses picked it up and gave it to me. You had already left.' I paused as she unfolded it and recognition drained the wry smile from her face. 'I thought you might need it.'

She swallowed, folded the paper again, and placed it on the desk next to her. She looked at me evenly. 'You read it, then,' she said, measuring me up.

'I was coming home from work so I thought I could just drop it off. It was no bother, so no need to thank me.' I turned to walk out of the room.

'Simon,' she called after me and her voice broke slightly, betraying her. I turned around. She wasn't looking at me but was looking at the cello between her legs, the window, the ceiling, anywhere but me. 'They don't know,' she said quietly, with weary resignation. 'And it's none of your business.' She looked back up at me, the aggravation creeping back into her voice.

I just looked at her calmly and answered her how she wanted me to. 'You're right; it's none of my business.'

I turned back towards the door, and as I walked away I heard her breathe out and place her bow on her desk. I walked down the stairs and into the kitchen, where Joanna was sitting with two glasses of water, waiting for me. She looked up at me and smiled.

It was none of my business. But that didn't mean I didn't care.

FIVE

Joanna

The sea stretched out in front of me, like a boundless blanket of turquoise waves, glistening like gems had fallen into it from the sun that shone above. I ran fast. The wind blew my hair back against my neck and the waves threw droplets against my ankles. It was still early and yet the sun was high in the sky. I ran faster. My beating heart deafened my whirling thoughts, and all I focused on was pushing in and out of the sinking sand beneath my feet and reaching the end of a beach that seemed infinite.

Simon hadn't stayed late last night. He seemed to have a lot on his mind. I thought he was working too hard.

I slowed down and came to a gradual stop. I rested my hands on my hips and bent over, trying to catch my breath. Once I had steadied my breathing I found a spot on a bit of grass poking out of the sand. I sat with one leg bent under the other, wiped my sweaty palms on my shorts and then leant back on my arms, sinking my hands deep into the sand. I closed my eyes and let the sun heat my eyelids.

After Simon left last night, Katrina went to bed early. She had been working on some new artwork all day and wanted to do more today, so she wanted an early night. Imogene stayed in her room for the rest of the evening, and Jason went to bed shortly after Katrina. I was flicking through channels on the TV when my phone rang. It was Abbey.

Apparently Charlie had gone out with a few people we knew from school. When she had called Abbey, apparently, she had passed well out of the range of comprehensibility. Abbey said she had been pretty upset, saying something about a guy she had met. It was definitely something about a guy, but Abbey said she couldn't make out what exactly had happened. I had got a few missed calls from Charlie around midnight, but when I had tried to return them she hadn't answered. Abbey said she had offered to pick her up, but Charlie just took herself home.

I would be lying if I said this kind of behaviour was a novelty from Charlie. It was like a recurring play; Abbey and I were the stage hands, and Charlie was the heroine whose life was wrapt with never-ending dramatic turmoil.

I pushed myself up and dusted the sand off my shorts and my legs. I let my gaze wander over the lapping waves to my right as I walked back up to the house. Abbey was coming over for lunch. Charlie was meant to come over too, but apparently this morning she was facing the consequences of last night. I couldn't help but laugh at it all. I was kind of jealous of Charlie's 'drama'. I think I would much prefer my worries to be concerned with drinking too much and what dress to wear that night.

I looked up as some birds flew overhead, their silhouettes standing out dramatically against the sky. My mum once said that if she could be any animal, it would be a bird. 'Just imagine the freedom of flight,' she said. My dad joked that the only benefit of being a bird would be the ability to crap on all your enemies and then fly away. Imogene had laughed at that, and I laughed now, remembering it. She then started listing the people she would crap on if she were a bird.

I watched as the birds settled on the sand ahead of me.

People did all sorts of things to try to set themselves free. I thought about Charlie. Maybe she was trying to escape something deeper than the simple dreariness of sobriety. Or maybe she just simply wanted to have fun.

But everyone wants to escape something. The difference is that all birds have to do is to spread their wings and fly. I asked myself, *Would I do it? If I could just spread wings and fly away, would I do it? Would I be able to say goodbye to it all?*

I walked up the path to my house; the path my dad had created using bits of scrap wood. As I got further up the path our back gate revealed itself, hidden under some overgrown ivy. I smiled, resigned, as I opened the gate: even if you could fly away, you can't escape what has already happened.

Jason greeted me as I walked into the house. 'You're really sweaty,' he said, crinkling his nose at me. He was at the table watching something on his phone. He squirmed and cried out when I flung my arms around him dramatically. 'You're so weird,' he said light-heartedly, as he looked back down at his phone.

'Is Imogene up?' I asked as I got myself a glass of water.

He shrugged. 'Don't know, don't care.'

I frowned, but the doorbell rang, interrupting my stream of thought.

I opened the front door and Abbey flung herself in, storming straight for the living room. I looked back at Jason in the kitchen and he raised his eyebrows at me.

'Good morning, Abbey. Come on in!' I laughed, shutting the front door. I walked into the lounge, where Abbey had collapsed onto one of the sofas. 'You know you're early?' I mused, leaning on the door-frame.

Jason came and stood next to me, befuddled.

She grunted and then sat up with her head resting back on the sofa cushion. 'After getting no sleep because of Charlie's dramatics, my parents then forgot to tell me that our kitchen is getting reconstructed today. I was woken up by the sound of drills and builders whistling in my kitchen.' She looked up at me completely unamused. 'Who whistles when other people are sleeping?'

'OK, note to self: Never whistle in your presence.' I looked down at my clothes. 'I need to go and shower and get dressed. Stay there and take a nap or something.'

'I need coffee,' she mumbled, closing her eyes.

I came downstairs about half an hour later, drying the ends of my hair with a towel as I walked into the lounge. Jason was sitting next to Abbey on the sofa. She had a mug of strong-smelling coffee in her hands, and he had a mug of what looked like orange squash. He was nodding knowingly, as she seemed to be filling him in on what happened last night. They both looked up as I walked in, trying my hardest not to laugh.

Jason held up a mocking finger to silence me before I could speak. 'Abbey, you are a strong, independent woman and I hear what you are telling me.'

'Jason, what are you…'

'You wouldn't understand, Joanna. This is adult talk,' he said in a superior tone.

Abbey choked on her coffee as she snorted with laughter. I threw a cushion at him playfully and then ushered him out of the room. All the while he complained that he was bored and wanted to hear the gossip. Two seconds later I heard him ascending the stairs, calling for Katrina.

I sat down and folded my legs under me. Abbey sat opposite me, still smiling. She was wearing a pale yellow T-shirt that complemented her skin tone nicely. Her copper hair hung in wild ringlets down to her waist. Her dad was Fijian, but her mum was English and she had inherited her fawn-coloured eyes.

As soon as I sat down we started discussing last night.

'She's done this before, though, it's hardly out of the ordinary,' I commented.

'I know,' Abbey agreed, resigned. 'But did Simon tell you

that she asked to meet him for coffee the other day?' she added eagerly.

'No, he didn't.'

'Oh,' she frowned, thinking deeply. 'Now that is weird. He probably just didn't think anything of it.'

'What was it about?'

'She didn't say. She just told me I couldn't come over because she was going out with Simon.'

'Maybe it was a date,' I laughed casually.

'Pft, as if it would be a date,' Abbey said incredulously, making a face. But then she paused and looked at me frowning, eyeing me up. 'It definitely wouldn't be a date... would it?'

I shrugged. I was never one for gossip, and I was always one to shy away from unnecessary drama. There was no point making a farce of the little things when life was enough of a show already. That was my thinking, at least, although my heart did seem to be beating a bit faster than normal. Abbey continued to eye me up suspiciously.

'Stop looking at me like that! Maybe she's in trouble with the law and needs his legal advice, or maybe they're running off to Vegas together to elope. Or maybe they were just having coffee,' I joked.

'The first option would definitely be the most interesting,' Abbey added drolly.

'I always thought Charlie had it in her to be a criminal.' I whipped around and Imogene was standing in the doorway, her arms folded across her chest. She was still wearing her pyjamas.

'I didn't know you were up.'

'I just woke up. I didn't mean to eavesdrop by the way. But I was at the coffee shop when they were there, and it would have to be a very cosy lawyer-client relationship,' she said, grinning.

I just shook my head and pushed my hair back behind my ear. 'This is ridiculous, guys.'

'Oh, I don't know, Jo,' Imogene said whimsically, her face mocking, 'you've strung Simon along for so long now, maybe he decided to hook up with the next best thing; the best friend.'

Heat rushed to my cheeks as though I was ten years old again. 'I haven't strung anyone along,' I said, through clenched teeth.

Abbey looked down awkwardly, pulling loose threads from a cushion.

'You never were the best judge of character, were you?' Imogene said patronisingly.

'Oh, I don't know about that! She's always complimenting me, and I am pretty fantastic,' Katrina said jovially, bursting in through the front door. 'You can ask Hugh Grant. I met him once and he said I had a lovely spirit.' Katrina stood in the doorway beside Imogene and looked into the room, assessing the situation she had just walked into. 'Abbey, how are you? How's your mum?'

'She's good, thanks,' she replied politely, glancing between the three of us. 'We're getting a new kitchen put in today.'

'Lovely!' Katrina paused and then turned to Imogene. 'Still terrorising the townspeople?'

I smiled, but the heat was still in my cheeks. Imogene laughed dryly.

'Who wants tea?' Katrina asked and we followed her out of the room. But she turned quickly and ran back to where Imogene was ascending the stairs. Abbey went to sit on a stool at the counter, but I stood by the door and looked back.

Katrina took a small white bag out of her handbag and handed it to Imogene. 'You left this in the car,' she said to her quietly.

It was a paper bag that you get from pharmacies, or at least that's what it looked like. Imogene looked uncomfortable as she took the bag and thanked Katrina. Katrina smiled up at her softly, and patted her arm before Imogene turned around and ascended the stairs.

'What was that about?' I asked her as she came into the kitchen.

She busied herself making three mugs of tea, and answered with her back to me. 'She has a bit of a cough so the doctor gave her some antibiotics,' she said, waving away the question with her hand. 'What were you all talking about before I interrupted?' she asked, smiling cheerfully as she looked at Abbey and I.

Abbey launched into retelling her all about Charlie, including the context of her recent break-up. Abbey wasn't to know, but this was probably unnecessary as I had kept Katrina up to date on everything since starting uni. Katrina poured hot water into the mugs of tea and listened attentively as Abbey filled her in, including how Imogene had just interrupted us.

Katrina laughed flippantly. 'Just ignore her,' she said placing the mugs on the counter in front of us. 'About Charlie: I would have thought you guys had outgrown this type of thing when you left school.' She raised her eyebrows at us and rubbed her forehead. 'She's obviously going through a bit of a rough time, and if last night is proof of anything it's that she's not quite sure how to deal with those emotions healthily,' she said knowingly, using her hands to make exaggerated gestures. She always did that when she was trying to keep a conversation light. 'Rather than speculating, why don't you just make sure you're there for her, as and when she needs you to be?'

Abbey shrugged and smiled sheepishly.

'Anyway,' Katrina continued, sipping her tea, 'we all know Simon prefers red hair to black.'

Abbey grinned and hid her face behind her hand.

'Enough!' I told them, exasperated.

Abbey stayed until later that afternoon. Katrina made us lunch and we took Jason down to the beach for a bit. Abbey told us all about an internship she was applying for, for next summer.

It was still hot but there were dark thunder clouds moving in across the sky; however, this only made it hotter for the time being. Tomorrow the clouds would break and drench the earth below. The birds danced on the water and Jason ran after the ones that lingered too long on the sand. Abbey left shortly after we got back to the house.

'Joanna,' Katrina called for me once I had shut the front door behind Abbey. She came out of the kitchen, drying her hands with a tea-towel. I was clenching and unclenching my left hand into a fist, as the scars had become more sensitive in the sun.

'What's up?'

'I didn't want to push the subject when Abbey was here,' she sighed, pausing. 'I know Imogene's tough. Well, tough might be an understatement. Just... don't go too hard on her.'

'What are you talking about?' I asked, unconvinced. 'I think you're talking to the wrong half of the duo here.'

She shook her head whimsically. 'You sounded so like your dad just then.' She sighed as I frowned at her, and then tried again. 'I am not saying in any way that you have done anything wrong...'

'Good.'

'I'm just saying, give her a bit more slack. The last thing I want is for her to keep pushing your buttons and then for you to finally snap. Sometimes we have to make a choice if we want to keep people in our lives. We have to decide how much we're willing to put up with. Don't let her push you to your limits.'

I took a second and looked carefully at my aunt. 'Why are you always so forgiving of her? Why don't you get angry? Why do you always go so easy on her? You know what she's like.'

I honestly couldn't remember the last time they had clashed like Imogene and I did.

She took my left arm in her hand, and in that split second, as she looked up at me, she had never looked so much like my dad.

'I also know that life takes its toll on people in different ways. We don't choose what happens to us but we can choose the compassion with which we treat people. Just don't give up on her, OK?'

I hesitated before responding. There was so much I wanted to say to Katrina, but at that point in time I seemed unable to articulate any of it. How do you argue with someone who's simply asking you to persevere with compassion?

'OK.' I turned and walked up the stairs.

SIX

Imogene

'*Run!*'

Joanna is standing directly in front of me. Her hair is dishevelled, matted with blood and sweat. Her body is on fire. Flames are crawling up her arm, concealing her scars. Behind her, a car is burning brightly, throwing amber and crimson flashes against a pitch black canvas.

'Why?' I ask her, my heart pounding so hard I barely hear the words escape my lips.

'Run or the flames will catch you too,' she whispers to me. A tear runs down her cheek, the colour of rust.

Without thinking I start to run.

I run into the darkness, trying to break through to consciousness, but I am trapped in the nightmare. I run further into the darkness.

Every few metres a mirror appears and I am obstructed by a reflection, forcing me to turn and run another way until another mirror appears, bearing another reflection that I can't quite make out. The flames behind me continue to reach for me, the heat clawing at my back and biting at my ankles.

'Imogene.'

I stop dead at the mirror in front of me. It is taller and wider than me, with a frame made from bits of scrap metal. I look closer and realise it's scrap metal from a car, and within its border stands the reflection of my mother.

'Imogene,' her reflection whispers to me in her soothing tone. She's so beautiful. I feel the tears flow steadily down my cheek.

'Mum, I'm sorry. Mum!' I scream.

I begin to claw at the mirror, but her reflection is moving further into the darkness, escaping me. I begin to beat the glass with my fists, trying to break her free.

There is a sharp squealing of tyres.

'*No!*' I yell.

The mirror explodes and I am thrown back onto a dirt floor. All around me the mirror is falling to the ground as ash.

Silence.

I clamber to my knees looking around frantically, my ears ringing from the force of the explosion. There's nothing there. I close my eyes and rub them hard. I open them and Simon is standing in front of me. He's standing in front of me with his hand outstretched. The ash continues to fall around him, covering his shoulders with the shadowy powder.

'I can't,' I whimper, shying away from his outstretched hand.

He kneels down and puts his hand on my shoulder. I look up at him. I take his hand, and he pulls me to the feet. He smiles at me, and turns me around.

'Mum,' I whisper. 'Dad.'

My parents are standing in front of me. I shake my head and close my eyes. I try to hold it in, but my sobs shake my body. The tears that flow down my cheeks turn to glass, shattering as they hit the floor.

'Please. Please, don't make me,' I sob.

'You have to let us go, Imogene,' my mother says, each word hitting my chest like a stone, threatening to throw me back to the floor. I close my eyes and shake my head. I feel her take my face in her hands and when I open my eyes her face is in front of mine. 'You have to say goodbye.'

I hear Jason cry out, but I can't see him. I look back at my mother.

'No,' I whisper, calmly, but without feeling.

My mother lets go of my face, her hands falling to her sides as she steps back. 'You have to let go of the pain, Imogene.' She walks further back to my father's side. 'Imogene, you have to say goodbye to the past, or you will never survive the life you are yet to live.'

I hear a cry again, but this time it is Joanna. My mother and father begin to fade, and I can see through them. Joanna and Jason stand hand in hand behind them, calling out for me.

'I don't know how to, Mum,' I weep, banging my head with my fists.

I try to turn my back on them, to scream that I don't even belong with them. But I can't. Instead I am forced to stand and watch as my parents disappear before my eyes. Joanna and Jason stand before me as they did nine years ago. Joanna holds her left arm in her right hand. The flames have died away and the scars remain.

Another explosion.

I jolted awake, panting hard. There was a knocking at my door. I looked around my room, thoroughly disorientated. I was covered in sweat, but I was awake. *I'm awake*, I told myself.

There was another gentle knock and Jason walked in. 'Katrina asked me to ask you what time you're going out tonight.'

'What?'

'What. Time. Are. You. Going. Out. Tonight?' he said again, exaggerating each word.

He was standing in my doorway, fully dressed, with a book in his right hand as his left still held the door handle.

He stared at me quizzically. 'Are you OK? Did you only just wake up? It's the afternoon.'

'Um, I don't know yet. Sometime around ten maybe,' I answered, swallowing even though my throat is dry. I pushed my hair back. I glanced at my clock. He was right, it was later than I had thought.

'OK.' He paused, watching me. 'Are you sure you're OK?'

'I'm fine,' I snapped at him. He turned away to walk out the door, rolling his eyes dejectedly. 'Jason,' I called and he turned back to face me. 'Thanks,' I said, and even I could hear how pathetic it sounded. He nodded, but he looked confused.

To say that I was shaken was a major understatement.

I took a deep breath and climbed out of bed. I took my time getting ready, letting the steam of the shower relax my muscles, taking time to blow dry my hair and actually pay attention to what clothes I was putting on. But it kept replaying in my head. I kept seeing them. Jason and Joanna reaching out for me, the fading image of my parents, the squealing of tyres, and an explosion. I usually slept dreamlessly, too tired to let my subconscious take a hold, but last night my subconscious had decided to break down the front door, spray the room with petrol and light a match. I didn't know how to deal with it. How did normal people deal with dreams like this?

I made myself breakfast and took it back to my room, where I spent the rest of the day. The exact details had begun to escape me but I still remembered a few things, with more clarity than I cared for: the squealing of tyres, an explosion, and Joanna's arm.

When it got to half past ten Mary texted me to tell me she was parked outside, ready to go. I grabbed my bag, and made my way downstairs. By the front door I stopped to check my appearance in the mirror. I had tied half of my hair up into a loose bun, and taken the time to apply my make-up with more care than I usually bothered with. I pursed my crimson-red lips and closed my eyes, one at a time, to check my eyeliner.

'I'm leaving!' I yelled up the stairs, grabbing my leather jacket from the banister and pulling it on.

Katrina yelled her goodbye back down the stairs.

'Where are you going?' Joanna emerged from the kitchen eating crisps from a bowl she was carrying in her hands.

I shrugged, 'Some friends from work are having a party.'

'Cool. Have fun,' she replied dryly, placing more crisps in her mouth as she turned towards the living room.

I gulped. 'Joanna,' I stammered.

'What?' She turned back around, frowning at me.

I hesitated and she tilted her head expectantly. I fiddled with the sleeve of my jacket, looking down. I wasn't used to feeling awkward. 'About the bonfire,' I began, and she rolled her eyes, but I kept going. 'I wanted to tell you that I'd think about it. Maybe it wouldn't be such a bad idea.' When I raised my eyes to look at her she wore the same look of confusion that Jason had.

Mary beeped her horn. 'I've got to go.' I offered her what I hoped was a kind smile as I left.

She smiled back at least, although she didn't look thoroughly convinced. I frowned as I walked down our front garden path. Was it really so hard to believe that I would do something, anything, nice? The corners of my mouth turned up in a bitter smile. *Yes*, I thought to myself.

People don't always understand the battles you are fighting within the confines of your mind; all they know are the arrows you rain down on them. They had no reason to give me the benefit of the doubt.

It was a short drive to the party. It was at a house closer to town that Theo was sharing with a couple of other guys. Mary talked the whole way there, so I just rested my head against the window and looked out at the pools of light the passing street lights were making on the ground, laughing here and there whenever socially appropriate.

When we arrived it was still relatively early but there was already a steady flow of bodies moving in and out of the house. The blaring music hit us as soon as we got out of the car.

'Imogene! Mary!' Theo yelled to us, emerging from the crowd. He wandered over to us, a drink in one hand, waving the other arm to stabilise his stride. Mary and I exchanged droll glances. When he got to us he threw one arm around my shoulder, roughly. I felt the weight of his body as he leant against me. 'When did you get here?'

'Five seconds ago,' I answered, freeing myself of his arm. He quickly put it back around me. 'But you've already started I can see,' I said wryly.

He smirked and then called a couple of his friends over to us. One of them was called Zeph. He was one of the guys who lived with Theo so I had met him quite a few times. The other I recognized as Frank, a guy who Theo had known from school. As soon as they reached the front step where we stood, Theo ushered us all inside to get drinks.

Someone grabbed hold of Mary as soon as we walked through the door, and dragged her off to a circle of excitable girls throwing their arms around her in delight. Meanwhile I was ushered into the kitchen with the boys. I made myself a drink and leant against the counter, sipping now and then. Theo and Frank were trying to sing along with the music blaring from speakers in the other room.

As the night went on more people arrived, the small rooms of the house got increasingly cramped, and the overall scene got messier. I loosened up as the night went on, and I began to move around the house, meeting up with different people as I went. Every now and then Theo would appear by my side, make sure I had a drink in my hand, and then wander off.

Everyone seemed in pretty good spirits. Usually I was amongst the best of them, but tonight I just didn't seem able to match any of them. I had been talking to Mary and a few guys from work when I decided I needed to get some air. I signalled to her that I was going outside for a minute and she nodded and blew me a kiss. I grabbed my jacket off one of the chairs and headed outside.

It was a cloudless night and the moon shone down on us between the roofs of the surrounding buildings. I wandered a short distance down the side of the house, so I wasn't standing directly by the door. I breathed out languidly when I saw that I was finally alone. I put down the still full drink I been holding and rested my head back against the cold concrete, closing my eyes.

'I thought I'd lost you then,' Theo said brashly, breaking into my haven from tonight's chaos. He never had been able to hold his drink.

'Keeping tabs on me?' I looked up at him as I remained where I was, leaning back. My head was spinning slightly.

He laughed brusquely and waved a hand in the air dismissively, but his eyes remained locked on my face. 'I just want to make sure you're having a good night.'

I laughed humourlessly and tilted my head at him. 'I'm having a blast. Which is why I came out here to be alone. I'll be back in a minute.'

'Why do you always have to do that, Imogene?' he said, his smile gone. He was standing right in front of me now. I glanced sideways and I could see people moving in and out of the house.

'Do what?' I asked, gritting my teeth as I grew increasingly aggravated.

He smiled broadly, superficially. 'You should be celebrating!' He said throwing his hands in the air. I stared at him, waiting for further explanation. 'I know, Imogene. I know you got the interview.'

I looked away from the pressure of his grin and pushed my hair back. 'I don't know what you're talking about. I've never mentioned anything about an interview.'

He laughed coarsely. 'You didn't have to. You couldn't possibly have thought the news wouldn't travel. Especially when you're friends with the very same people you beat to get it.'

'Of course.' I sighed cynically. 'Why didn't you tell me you had applied?'

'Did you think you were the only one destined for success? New York, Imogene!' His drink sloshed about erratically. He sighed dramatically and tilted his head at me, his glazed eyes appraising me. 'You were just the only one cut-throat enough to actually get an interview.'

I looked away from him towards the moon. I could only just make it out through the tall bushes that lined the side of the house where we stood. He laughed again, bringing my gaze back to him.

'Have you told that delightfully screwed-up family of yours that you're abandoning them, then?'

I scrunched up my face in disgust as I rolled my eyes, and stood up from the wall, dusting off my jeans. 'I'm not in the mood for your bullshit, Theo. Get out of my way.' He had moved sideways so that he was blocking my way to the house. 'Move,' I said, my tone biting. He just smiled at me and titled his head mockingly to one side.

I went to push past him but he grabbed my arm abruptly and shoved me back. I fell against the wall and scraped my hand. I got straight back up and darted to his left. He was holding his drink in that hand, and he threw the glass to the floor. I felt the liquid splash against my legs. He grabbed my arm with his newly freed hand and pulled me around to face him.

'You're more pathetic than I thought,' he whispered, holding me close to him.

I could feel the tears stinging my eyes. I ripped my arm free, put both of my hands on his chest and shoved, hard.

He stumbled back and tripped over, falling against the wall. I turned and walked quickly back up to the house, but rather than going in, I turned to walk down the path to the road. The bitter tears were falling freely down my cheeks now. I put my hands in my pockets to find my phone. I'd tell Mary I wasn't feeling well, that I had to go home.

'What a mess.'

I looked up, freeing my hands from my jacket pockets. 'Charlie?'

Joanna's friend was standing a little way off from the path, walking away from a group who were huddled near the driveway. She stood on the path opposite me with her hands folded in front of her. She was wearing a crimson red playsuit that stood out starkly against her translucent skin and the long black hair that hung over her shoulder. I could only just see her from the bits of light that streamed out from the house.

'What are you doing here?' I asked.

'Having a better time than you, by the looks of it,' she laughed looking me over. 'You really are a mess, aren't you.'

'And you really are a bitch, aren't you,' I threw back, glaring at her as tears dropped off my chin. I gulped, shaking my head as I smiled crookedly. 'Then again, Joanna never did like you as much as the others.'

Her mocking smile broke into a sneer. It was true, she had never been as bubbly as Abbey, or as kind as Leo, but as I looked at her sneering at me, as make-up and tears washed down my face, I had never seen her look so poisonous.

'Joanna was right. You are pathetic. I would say that being a wreck runs in the family, but that would be a bit impossible to prove in your case, wouldn't it.' She tilted her head and flashed her white teeth in a sardonic smile.

My stomach flipped at the shock of her venomous words. "Fuck you."

I shook my head and stormed away from her, as fresh tears

escaped my eyes. I didn't want her to see me crying. I didn't want her to see how much of a wreck I really was.

'Imogene!'

I glanced back, and Simon was walking down the pavement towards me.

I guffawed, shaking my head despairingly as I continued to walk away. Where were they all coming from?

'Leave me alone!' I yelled back, my quivering voice betraying me.

SEVEN

Simon

'Simon, you came!'

'What the hell was that, Charlie?' I asked, indicating the road Imogene had just stormed down as I walked over to where Charlie stood.

She guffawed, playing with a strand of her hair. 'You know what Imogene's like.' She sighed and smiled broadly. 'She started going mental, saying all this horrible stuff about Joanna, and I told her to stop. She only got angrier, of course, and stormed off before I could calm her down. You can ask any of them.' She indicated to a group of guys swaying behind her. One guy had his eyes closed and was singing to himself.

'Those guys are wasted, Charlie.' I shook my head and looked to where Imogene had walked off. I looked back at Charlie. She stood staring at me expectantly. 'You called me, saying it was an emergency?'

'It is,' she said, smiling as she took my arm in her hand. 'You have to come get a drink with me.'

'You have got to be kidding, Charlie,' I snapped, taking my arm from her hand. 'I...' I couldn't finish what I was saying as I was too angry. I sighed, trying to compose myself. 'You called me saying you needed help.'

'Well, that was just to get you down here,' she replied, her smile fading in her disappointment.

'I'm going to make sure Imogene doesn't end up in a ditch somewhere.' I turned, walking the way Imogene had gone. 'Enjoy the rest of your night!' I yelled back to her, waving my hand in the air sarcastically.

It was a cloudless night and the moon shone down on the pavement before me. I picked up the pace and started to jog as the cold summer night air began to creep under my hoodie. I didn't have to go far.

I rounded a corner and came to one of the entrances to the park. I noticed the gate swinging open so I took my chances and went through. The park was eerily quiet. The streetlights provided intermittent light, and birds were singing their night songs hidden within the trees and bushes. I had walked less than a minute when I saw her slumped on a bench. She was leaning forward with her face in her hands, sobbing gently. The moonlight mingled with the lingering light of the flickering street lamp, throwing her miserable shadow against the path in front of her.

I went and sat beside her on the bench and rested my hands on the cool wooden seat. She turned her head, and as recognition flooded her eyes the tears began to flow stronger. She sighed earnestly, throwing her head back to look at the sky above. She didn't bother to wipe her eyes, but let her emotions lie plainly painted on her face.

For a couple of minutes we sat in silence. She continued to look at the sky, breathing deeply as her sobs began to ease. I looked at the park in front of me, trying to find the calling birds in the blanket of darkness before me.

'You didn't have to come after me, you know,' she said after a while, looking at me with that crooked grin she so often wore. But her smile quickly faded, and she frowned down at her hands clasped in her lap.

'I probably wouldn't be able to live with myself if you got kidnapped or something,' I said wryly, watching her as I leant back.

She laughed gently. 'Always the knight in shining armour,' she smiled, leaning back to look at me properly.

'What happened, then? Don't make me rely on Charlie for information. Her reliability has kind of been called into question tonight,' I told her, my voice still bitter.

She made a noise of disgust at the mention of Charlie's name. She looked back at me, her stark blue eyes piercing in the dim light. 'Why are you even here?'

'I tell you, and you tell me?'

'OK,' she said smiling again, not sadly but with a certain intimacy that I had never seen in her before.

So I told her how Charlie had tricked me with the pretence of an emergency. She laughed loudly, and mocked me once again as a 'knight in shining armour'. I told her that after being woken up at 2 a.m. I might try being the villain next time.

Then she told me everything. It took far longer than my story had; she broke down so easily.

She began by telling me about her dream, and then she told me about Theo and Charlie, and her confrontations with them both. I was disappointed to hear that Charlie had had a role to play in causing the tears that now marked her face. Once she had told me how she came to be in the park, she backtracked. She told me about New York.

She had applied for a job at a small studio in New York that worked with a lot of classical musicians. They had got back to her last week and asked her to meet them next week for an interview. If the interview went well and she got the position, she would then be moving to New York for one year at the end of the summer. If the year went well, then who knows how long she would be out there. It was the chance of a lifetime, everything she had ever wanted, and yet she wasn't happy.

'You haven't told them, have you?' I asked as it dawned on me.

She shook her head and looked at me, her eyes searching

mine. She wiped her face roughly with the back of her hand. As she pulled her hair loose from its bun her blonde curls fell down her back and a few strands swung around her face. She didn't bother to push them back.

She opened and closed her mouth a few times before the words finally escaped her lips in a whisper. 'I can't leave them, Simon.'

I looked down at my feet, scuffing the ground in front of me with my shoe. 'They would want you to go. They would want you to be happy,' I finally said, solemnly. It was too simplistic, but I didn't know how to give advice to Imogene. I didn't know her.

She sighed. A few more seconds passed and something rustled in the undergrowth behind us.

When she looked back at me her expression startled me. Fresh tears were rolling down her face, causing unruly strands of hair to cling to her cheeks. The tears in her eyes made the irises look as if they were dancing on a sea of tempestuous waves.

'I can't leave them!' she said again, this time her voice rising louder, almost hysterical.

'Except, they're not the reason you would be staying, are they?' I asked her, remembering the letter that had fallen from her bag. I kept going, speaking slowly, 'You don't want to leave because you don't think you can.'

'Ask me. I know you want to,' she told me, a sardonic smile breaking onto her lips.

I didn't bite. 'No.' I clasped and unclasped my hands as I watched her. I was out of my depth, but I hoped the calmness of my voice was reflected on my face. 'Imogene, you are lucky enough to still have people who care about you. When…' I breathed out, trying to stay placid. 'When you have thrown it back in their faces, those people have stayed put and tried again and again to be there for you. What do you think they would want you to do? Don't you think they want you to go, and to do what makes you proud?'

'You still don't get it.'

'Explain it to me, then.'

She stood up quickly from the bench. Pacing back and forth on the path, she clawed back her hair and held her head in her hands. All of a sudden she stood still and looked back at me, her hands on her hips, dancing back and forth nervously on the balls of her feet. She sighed.

'Explain to me why you haven't told them you're depressed.'

She shook her head repeatedly, and began pacing back and forth again. 'I don't want them to know how broken I really am.' She said it breathing out, as if she were expelling these words from her very being. She came to an abrupt standstill. She didn't sound angry, she didn't sound sad. She was tired. She rolled her head backwards to look up at the stars above and let her arms fall to her side.

Then she came to sit back down next to me, slumping beside me, shaking her head softly. I wondered how long she had been waiting to tell someone, anyone, what she was telling me.

'I can't go to New York because I can't say goodbye to them. I can't leave them. I'm sure they would sooner see the back of me, but I need them, Simon. I was first diagnosed after the accident. But the funny thing about depression is that you're never really cured. My doctor put me on some medication again recently, and Katrina's been trying to get me to talk to someone. That's the letter you found: a referral.

'I wish I could explain to you what it's like,' she whispered. 'It's like someone's screaming inside my head, all day, every day, trying to block out everything else. Like my entire world is crumbling down around me, and the rubble is just piling up upon my shoulders, threatening to bring me to my knees any minute.

'Jason's *twelve years old*, Simon. Joanna's started uni. At least Jason can't remember the accident, he was too young. Joanna does. She's got her own battles to fight without trying to fight mine as well.

'You think I'm a bitch. I know you do. I don't blame you, if I'm honest. Sometimes being a villain is easier than being a victim. I isolate myself from them. I yell, I block them out, I tell them I don't belong with them, that I'm not really their sister. I hurt them because I'm afraid the minute I let them in they will know just how loudly I've been screaming for help. They've lost their parents. They don't need to know they're losing their sister as well. It terrifies me, Simon.' She drifted off, her lips trembling as the tears dropped off of her chin.

I had no idea what to say. All this time, I had had no idea that her scars went this deep; no idea what had been going on inside her mind. I had never bothered to ask.

'They haven't lost their sister,' I finally said quietly, putting my hands on my legs and straightening my back.

She stood up suddenly, straightening her jacket roughly with her shaking hands. 'We should go,' she sighed, and without another word she started walking towards the park gate.

I decided to walk Imogene home, rather than offering to drive us. I didn't want to disturb her once she started walking determinedly ahead. We walked in silence for most of the way. Imogene had stopped crying, and as we walked she looked around, watching the night as it moved around us. I put my hands in my pockets and walked silently beside her.

The day I first met Imogene, I must have been about six or seven years old. Joanna had invited me to her house after school. I struggled to remember, but I think my mum was in the kitchen chatting to Vera. Imogene ran into the room where

Joanna and I were playing. In my memory, she wore the same crooked grin. We played together for the rest of the afternoon, and when my mum told me it was time to go, Imogene was the one begging for us to stay longer. The three of us spent so much time together when we were younger. Yet it was only now that I was remembering it. It's bizarre how you can know someone for so long, and yet not really *know* them.

We rounded the corner onto her street and before we knew it we were at her driveway.

She stopped and looked at me uncertainly. 'You won't...'

'I won't tell anyone,' I told her before she could finish.

The corners of her mouth lifted up subtly. She turned and walked away, reaching into her bag for her keys.

'Go to the interview,' I said quickly. She turned to look at me, her forehead furrowed. 'Even the villain needs a happy ending,' I laughed, cringing at my pathetic attempt to be wise and witty.

She smiled. 'Go home, Simon.'

'Good night, Imogene.'

I walked home slowly. My head was swimming. Who knew my story would have led to my consoling Imogene, of all people?

When I got home my mum's car was parked in the driveway but all of the lights were off. I tried to be as quiet as possible as I locked the door behind me and walked down the hall to my room. I got into my room and closed the door quietly, before slumping on my bed.

On the chest of drawers opposite my bed was a small, dark oak bookshelf. I looked at a photo of my dad in its blue frame. My mum had given it to me when I was younger. It was on the day that I had gone to Joanna's to play, the day I had met Imogene.

You may never know every word of someone's story, but that doesn't mean your name isn't written amongst the pages.

EIGHT

Jason

'Done,' I said to myself, satisfied. I closed the book and held it in my hands for a moment, revelling in my achievement. 'I finished another one!' I called down the stairs to whoever happened to be within hearing distance.

'Good job, Jason!' Katrina called back, her distant voice carrying throughout the house.

I smiled to myself as I pushed up from where I had been sitting on my bed. I walked over to my bookshelf. It sat in the corner of my room, but its contents overflowed onto the floor, forming piles. On top of the bookshelf, stacked neatly, were the books which Simon had lent me. I added this one to the pile and ran my finger over the remaining titles I had yet to read. I couldn't wait to talk to him about the ending of the one I had just finished, and yet I was already eager to begin the next story.

My room was the largest in the house. It was the only room on the third floor, with the roof slanting abruptly inwards on both sides. It was used for storage before I came along, but Joanna told me Mum renovated it when I was born. The walls hadn't been repainted since, but remained a pale yellow that caught the sun as it fell through the windows.

Next to my bookshelf sat a desk, with notebooks and pen pots carefully aligned on the back edge. On the wall above the desk was the photo collage Joanna and her friends made for my birthday. In the centre of the collage was a black and white photo of the family, taken just after I was born. My dad was holding me, and my mum was standing next to him with her hands on Imogene's and Joanna's shoulders. Next to that photo was one of Imogene giving me a piggy-back at the beach with Joanna running alongside us. That's the thing about photos; they capture the moments memory can't hold on to.

I didn't really remember them, but Mum and Dad looked happy enough in the photos.

I looked back to the bookshelf, thinking that I would like to write stories when I was older. In books, if the story gets too sad, or something happens that you don't like, you don't have to read on. You can close the cover and stay lost in the plot of the previous pages. However, I had never been one to not finish a book. I took the book that was next in the pile and shut my door behind me.

'Jerry!' I called as I descended the stairs to the ground floor. 'Jerry, here boy!'

I went into the kitchen and looked out of the window, but I couldn't see him. Jerry was our Bearded Collie. He was the family dog, but I was unequivocally his favourite. He usually disappeared to various parts of the house for most of the day, and then would eventually turn up to be fed and patted on the head.

I strolled to the lounge with the book held loosely in my right hand.

'Joanna, have you seen Jerry?' I asked her as she sat on the sofa, a mug in one hand and her phone in the other. 'How's Simon?' I asked grinning, nodding to her phone. 'Tell him he needs to come over. I need to talk to him about *The Book Thief.*'

'Have you tried the garden?' she asked, ignoring my request, but smiling nonetheless as she tilted her head towards me.

'Yeah. He's not there.'

'Maybe Katrina left the front door open again?'

'Hm, maybe. I'll check,' I replied as I left the room. It had happened countless times before, so wasn't unlikely. 'Jerry!' I called again, walking out of the front door and making my way down the drive.

A distant bark met my call.

It was warm outside, but a thin layer of cloud blanketed the sky, masking the sun. I rolled up my sleeves as I walked to the end of the driveway. I stood where our drive met the road, turning my head left and right to find the source of the bark.

Another bark sounded. It seemed to be coming from Mrs Vincent's house. That was weird, because they didn't have a dog: It must be Jerry.

'Did you find him?' Joanna asked, appearing at the front door with her arms folded across her chest.

'I can hear barking, but it sounds like it's coming from Mrs Vincent's.'

'Well, let's go and look,' she said, closing the front door behind her, and slipping her phone into the front pocket of her jeans.

Walking onto Mrs Vincent's property was like walking into a secret garden from one of my books. The rickety old gate squeaked when Joanna swung it open. Lining the pathway to the front door were hydrangea bushes, swelling with an abundance of purple and blue flowers. Roses, lavender and other varieties of flowers covered every other inch of the ground. Two stone bird baths rose from the centre of green bushes on either side of the path.

'Jerry!' I said in delight, as he came bounding over to me. Kneeling down to stroke him, I looked up to see where he had come from. Mrs Vincent's front door swung open, revealing the hallway beyond.

Joanna went inside. 'Mrs Vincent?'

I followed after her along the path, clicking for Jerry to follow me, which he did obediently.

'Jason!' Joanna's voice called, quick and firm.

My head shot up, accompanied by a simultaneous bark from Jerry. He ran ahead of me, gliding through the open door, and I quickly followed him, the grip on my book subconsciously tightening.

Once I had got through the front door, a dusty aroma greeted me, and I looked about, turning in a circle where I stood. I heard voices in the room to my left and so placing one hand flat on the door I pushed it open, sticking my head round the corner. 'Joanna?' I asked nervously.

Mrs Vincent was lying on the floor, favouring her right side as her left arm reached down her leg towards her ankle. Her face was crinkled in pain, but she seemed to be trying to wave Joanna away. Next to where Joanna knelt over Mrs Vincent, a stool lay fallen on the floor surrounded by what looked like soil. I quickly noticed the broken flower pot, from which its contents had been thrown.

'Oh, I'm fine. I just took a little tumble,' Mrs Vincent said dismissively, clutching Joanna's extended arm all the same.

'Jason, take her other arm and help me lift her into the chair. She's hurt her ankle.'

I did as Joanna instructed, discarding my book on one of the many bookshelves that towered about the room.

Sighing, Mrs Vincent gave me her arm and together Joanna and I helped her to her feet. Supporting most of her weight, we then helped her into a nearby armchair. Once in the chair she took off the shoe on her left foot and proceeded to massage her foot.

'Thank you both,' she said, amused, although her eyebrows still frowned in apparent pain.

'No problem,' Joanna said, standing back slightly and

placing her hands on her hips in a parental manner. 'We never would have come in if Jerry hadn't wandered off again.'

Mrs Vincent laughed roughly. 'That dog of yours is a wanderer.'

As we all turned to look at him, all we saw was his tail escaping back out of the door. I looked after him, grinning, and Mrs Vincent shook her head as she snickered. Joanna rolled her eyes, amused.

'Stay with Mrs Vincent, Jason, while I put Jerry back in the house.'

She broke into a half-run, calling after our illusive dog.

I turned back to Mrs Vincent who looked up at me benevolently.

'Where's Mr Vincent?' I asked politely, remaining where I stood.

'One of the nurses took him out for the day.'

'That's nice,' I nodded, looking around the room. 'Is your ankle OK? I sprained my ankle once. Joanna bounced me off the trampoline accidently. It hurt a lot. Does yours hurt?'

'It's nothing a tough woman like myself can't handle,' she said, smiling crookedly, although she continued to massage her ankle.

I patted my hands against my thighs rhythmically as I turned to pace the room. This room was dimmer than the entrance hallway, and made more so by the dark oak of the many bookshelves, and the dark brown leather armchairs. White net curtains blocked out most of the light from the large windows looking out over the front garden. The only other light source was a light bulb that hung from the ceiling.

'I like your library. I don't think I've ever been in this room before.' I ran my hand over the titles I didn't recognise, which were many.

'Oh, you have. Only when you were little, though. Your

father used to bring you in here when he would talk with Robert.'

'Is it his library? Robert's?'

'It is ours. Although he has come to favour this room more than myself. I prefer the garden, personally.' She paused, looking around the room fondly. 'Joanna tells me Simon has been lending you books?'

'Yep. I'm trying to read as much as I can this summer, so he's been giving me books he thinks I'll like.'

'And are you enjoying your summer?'

I nodded, and turned to another bookshelf. This one seemed to be full predominantly of thrillers and crime novels.

'You must be enjoying having Joanna home for the summer?'

I nodded and shrugged again. 'Do you have any historical fiction novels? They're my favourite.'

'That bookshelf,' she pointed to the one in the far right-hand corner, by the door. 'You do remind me of him,' she laughed gently.

'Of who?' I asked as I examined the shelf in front of me.

'Your dad, Benson.'

I shrugged again and returned to my examinations. 'Imogene says I look like him.'

'She's right. But I was referring to his countenance, not his appearance.'

Joanna was taking her time taking Jerry to the house.

'You can borrow anything you want.'

'Thanks!' I smiled appreciatively.

'That reminds me, actually. On that bookshelf over there, is a copy of *Gulliver's Travels* by Jonathan Swift. Could you get it down for me, please?'

I walked to the shelf she had pointed to, and climbing onto the first shelf reached up to where I spotted the requested title.

I took it down, grunting with the effort of reaching my hand up so high.

'Not for me, for you,' she said, as I went to hand it to her. I pursed my lips, confused, but opened the front cover.

My mouth fell open slightly. 'Why do you...'

'Robert found the copy for him. Benson was going to give it to you on your birthday,' she interrupted me. 'Robert found it the other day. He said he had put it away with the intention of giving it to its rightful owner at a later point.' She put her ankle back on the floor, and as she felt her temples with her fingertips a tired smile crossed her features. 'He told me to give it to you now, in case he never got to.'

I looked back at her, clutching her gift in my hands. I frowned, stuttering, 'Mrs Vincent, Joanna said Robert forgets things. That he's getting worse.'

'Alzheimer's, Jason, is a nasty bugger,' she said calmly, placing her hands on the arms of the chair on which she sat. A kind smile on her face, she watched me intently.

'Does he still remember who you are?' I asked, curiosity outweighing the required subtleties of politeness.

'Now and then.'

'But what if he doesn't? What if he doesn't remember who you are?' I asked again, rather more rhetorically. Avoiding her curious gaze I walked over to where I had left my book and, picking it up, placed it on top of my dad's.

'Your parents?'

I didn't turn to look at her but simply nodded.

'Memory is a trick, Jason. Whether or not you can recall a memory is not as important as people make out. It's how we live the influence that others have had on us. Who's to stop you from creating your own memories of your parents?'

'What do you mean?' I asked turning to look at her. 'They're dead.'

'I do know that Jason. I'm not the Vincent with

Alzheimer's,' she chuckled, 'at least not yet. What I mean is, let that book be your memory,' she continued, pointing to the copy in my hands. 'Let every word, of every page, breath to life a new memory of them. Let their memory live on in how every character influences you. You may not remember your parents from the past, but what's to stop you from remembering them in all you do in the future? There are no bystanders in life, Jason. Your parents have influenced you in ways you will never know. Therefore you, my boy, are a living memory.'

I stood frowning as I tried to fully understand what she was telling me. 'Thank you,' I said sheepishly, 'for the book.'

To my surprise she chuckled again. 'Don't look so serious. We would all be on our knees if we carried the weight on our shoulders that you look like you're carrying.'

I continued to frown at her, but even so, a smile curled up the corners of my lips. She was a weird old woman.

'Tell you what,' she proceeded, leaning forward on her elbows. 'I need a little help this summer organising this library, and in return you can borrow whatever takes your fancy. What do you say?'

'Deal!' I agreed, perking up.

'What do you say, Joanna? Sound like a good deal?' she called, raising her eyebrows at the door.

Joanna appeared through it, looking slightly sheepish as she smiled shyly. 'Sounds fair enough to me.'

Well that explains why she has taken so long, I thought.

'I didn't want to interrupt,' she explained, as she walked across the room to hand Mrs Vincent an ankle support bandage.

'Thank you, dear,' she said appreciatively, taking the bandage from Joanna. 'And what about you, Joanna? What are you doing with yourself this summer?'

She shrugged. 'Not much. Mostly spending time with people while I'm back.'

'So you're free to help me in my garden then? Brilliant,' Mrs Vincent said emphatically.

Joanna's face fell slightly, but Mrs Vincent broke into a grin, and Joanna sighed in sheepish relief.

NINE

Joanna, Present Day

My throat was dry. I kept trying to swallow but the sensation was like dragging velcro against sandpaper.

I winced as I tried to move around. There was a splitting pain in my head. I instinctively tried to reach up my hand but the effort proved too much. Over my hands lay a soft material. Blankets? The pain shot across the back of my head again.

I tried to open my eyes, but everything seemed clouded. I couldn't quite tell if my eyes were open or not. Noises began to sound, breaking past the dull ringing in my ears. I heard voices, but whose they were remained a mystery.

'Is she waking up?' one voice said.

'She's going to be fine. It was a pretty nasty hit, so just give her time,' another said.

Time.

I gave in to the darkness again. Tiredness broke me. I let the dreams blanket my clouded vision once more.

'Imogene?' She is standing in front of me on the beach, a crooked grin brightening her face as sunlight bounces off the waves before us. Her golden hair is illuminated, her laughing eyes piercing the glow with their electric blue.

'Imogene, what happened to me?'

She doesn't answer. Turning her face away from me she smiles towards the sea, inhaling the salty air.

'You don't remember, do you?' she asks me.

Screaming, crying, a blazing pain biting my left arm, and the policeman's fluffy grey hair.

'Remember what?' I ask, growing increasingly distressed. I grab my left arm, but quickly release it as my hands shoot up to my head. I hear more voices, but as I spin around, my feet throwing sand into the air, I see that the beach is deserted. It's just Imogene and I.

'I remember!' I yell at her, the pain in my head growing unbearable. 'I remember the accident! I remember the crash!'

There is a screeching sound, wheels on tarmac. Heat rises up my body as if the sand beneath is turning into flames threatening to consume me.

'Remember who the real knight in shining armour was?' Imogene asks me.

I turn, my hands falling from my head. We are surrounded by darkness, but against the pitch-black canvas is an all too familiar scene.

'I don't want to see this,' I say quietly, my voice surprisingly devoid of all emotion.

'You have to remember, little sister.'

Screaming, crying, a blazing pain biting my left arm, and the policeman's fluffy grey hair.

It plays out before my eyes like a slow-motion film. Two cars collide, and with it the lives of those within. Glass is smashed, blood spilled and fire ignited. But survivors stumble free of the storm of destruction.

'No. That's not right,' I whisper. The pain of my head

almost throws me back as it strikes my nerves with all its force. But I ignore it, the nightmare I have been thrown into spinning around me.

'Imogene, you pulled me from the car. You got me and Jason out! This isn't right!' I tell her, pointing in confusion at the lie seeking to unveil itself as truth.

The wicked smile painted on the face of the Imogene next to me curls into one more pointed, as despairing tears roll down her pale skin. She shakes her head. 'You were my knight in shining armour, Joanna. So, now it's my time to be yours.'

'I was so young. There's no way I could have got you two out safely. You pulled me from the wreckage before the whole car exploded. You saved me!'

'Memory is a powerful thing. But so is the emotion of our imagination.' Her smile fades. 'You were the hero, Joanna. You were my little sister. You wanted to believe that I was strong enough. You wanted to believe that I could protect you. So you distorted the truth.'

'I don't understand,' I say, angrily. Why would my mind lie to itself?

She walks away from me, watching my face all the while.

Everything seems to spin, the blackness threatening to engulf us once again. The pain in my head throws me to my knees, the ringing causing my head to spin, as my body seems to throw itself in circles.

'Simon,' I gasp, remaining on my knees as I fail to find my balance. 'Jason?'

I spin around and there they all are. Forming a loose semi-circle around me, Simon, Jason and Imogene stand in front of me.

'What's going on?' The ringing in my ears lessens and I hold my left arm, my scars hot to the touch.

I get to my feet, grunting with the effort. I try to force my consciousness to break me free of this nightmare. The voices are getting louder, clearer.

'Why are you here?' I ask, fear rising up in me. I don't understand it, but as I direct this question at Simon I feel like I already know the answer, that my mind is taunting itself.

He's always there.

I walk towards him so that my face is directly in front of his. 'You weren't involved in that accident, so why are you here?'

He takes my face in his hands, and I lean into his warmth. He smiles at me, but it only makes my panic grow. Then I notice it. There is blood on his shirt.

'It's like Mrs Vincent said,' Jason explains, as my attention focuses on him in my confusion. 'It's about remembering the acts of the past in how we live in the future. You saved us then. Now it's your turn to be saved.'

'No. Jason, no. I didn't even know it was me that pulled you out of the car!' I yell, exasperated.

'Everybody plays a part,' Imogene says, taking my hand in hers. She smiles kindly, but I shake my head in disbelief and despairing panic.

'You're bleeding,' I whisper.

She smiles once more, with her wry grin.

The ringing in my ears grows. The pain in my head worsens, and with the screeching of car wheels I am thrown from them all.

'Joanna? Joanna, honey, can you hear me?' Katrina asked me. I could feel her stroking my hair.

'Water,' I choked. 'Can I have water, please?'

'Of course. Hold on,' she said, the relief in her voice plain.

I blinked my eyes slowly. The cloud that blurred my vision broke into contrasting colour.

'What happened?' I ask, my voice croaky.

I moved myself up in the bed so that I was in more of a sitting position. I was in a hospital room.

'Here,' she said, handing me a plastic cup of water.

I took it and drank slowly. She sat down on the side of my bed. She looked tired, with dark shadows under her eyes, and deep lines formed on the centre of her forehead.

'Thanks.'

The icy cold water felt good, and I took a deep breath as I held the cup. I looked around the room, still disoriented, and then I felt the pain in the back of my head. I looked at my arm, panic suddenly rising up in me, but the scars were old, and cold beneath my touch. I breathed out, realising that I had been holding my breath.

'What happened?' I ask again.

'What do you remember?' she asked calmly, pushing strands of her erratic hair out of her face.

'I don't know.' I blinked harder, reality overtaking the nightmare I had just broken from, but neither clearer than the other. 'The anniversary…' my voice drifted off as I looked to Katrina for assurance. 'We were at the house.'

I tried to remember more, but frowned as the effort hurt my head. I rested my head back into the soft pillow, frustrated.

'It's OK. Take your time.'

She held my hands in hers. But something about her comforting smile put me on edge.

'Where is everyone?' Katrina was the only other person in this quiet hospital room. 'Where are Imogene and Jason?'

'Let me get a doctor,' Katrina said brusquely, rising from the bed. 'He asked me to get him when you woke up.'

'Katrina.' I say her name firmly, but panic was undeniably rising within me. She stayed standing with her back to me, looking as if she was ready to bolt for the door. '*What happened*?'

She turned to face me, her smile faded, tears in her eyes.

'There was an accident,' she explained, her hands clasping. She swallowed, trying to remain calm.

I felt the blood drain from my face. My breathing quickened, threatening to suffocate me.

'Katrina,' I pleaded. 'Where are they?'

TEN

Imogene, Two Months Earlier

My phone started ringing, yet again. Theo. I rolled my eyes, and clicked the 'decline' button before shoving my phone into my chosen black bag.

I can't be late.

I sat on my bed revising my notes, but I couldn't relax into this revision. I kept glancing up at the clock on the wall.

I had taken Simon's advice and accepted the interview for the position in New York. My lips clamped tightly together, and my feet tapped my bedroom floor as I struggled with the nerves seeking to bewilder me. I sighed. *Why am I doing this?* I thought to myself.

I hadn't spoken to Simon since that night. I hadn't really spoken to anyone since that night. At work the next day Mary asked what had happened to me. I told her about Theo. She called him an asshole, gave me a hug, and we hadn't spoken about it since. He kept calling, kept trying to talk to me, kept trying to apologise. It wasn't as though I had never seen that side to him before. But my conversation with Simon replayed itself clearly in my mind.

I couldn't screw up this time. Anyway, there was no guarantee I would get the position, and even if I did, I didn't necessarily have to take it. I laughed to myself and buried my head in my hands.

Did he have to be such a know-it-all?

I checked the clock again. It was almost time to leave. I got up from my bed, and collecting my notes together along with a small notebook and pen I filled my bag. I could hear my phone vibrating again, so I took it out and turned it to silent. Walking towards the door I paused by my mirror. A gentle rain was pattering against my window.

In the corner of the mirror I saw the reflection of my cello, its case lying on my bed. When he was younger Jason scrawled my name across the case in blue paint. I told him it looked better that way. I looked back to my own reflection, smiled, and shook my head.

I had heard him leave the house earlier in the morning. He seemed to be spending a lot of time at Mrs Vincent's house lately. I didn't really understand why, but Joanna had always had a soft spot for our neighbour and now it seemed Jason had joined the club. Like sister, like brother, I guess.

I knew he was still out and Katrina was at work so as I closed the door to my room and headed downstairs I knew it was Joanna I would have to slip by. I heard her bustling about in the kitchen.

'Nice blazer,' she said, perplexed but nonchalant. 'You're not usually this dressed up for work.'

I busied myself around the kitchen, filling my coffee flask. 'That's because I'm not going to work,' I said brusquely, pouring boiling water into the flask.

She cleared her throat, as she sat on one of the kitchen stools with her sandwich in front of her. 'Are you going to tell me where you're going, then?' she asked suspiciously, looking back and forth from her plate to where I stood facing the wall.

'I have an interview,' I said quickly, my effort to be casual failing. I felt the school of butterflies in my stomach break free.

She raised her eyebrows and then just as quickly frowned. 'An interview for what?'

I sighed. I put the lid on my flask and looped my other arm through my bag handle. 'What do most people have interviews for, Joanna? A job.'

'Well I'm sure you'll win them over with your wonderful charm,' she mumbled sarcastically. I couldn't help but smile; she sounded like Katrina. Her expression lightened as she noticed my smile. She looked down shyly. 'Good luck,' she said sincerely.

I looked down at the floor, pausing. 'Thank you,' I replied in a way in which I hoped matched her sincerity. I cleared my throat and started towards the front door.

He wouldn't have told her anything, I know he wouldn't have. But as I got into my car and drove into town, I wondered how he couldn't. If you knew something that would make life easier for someone you loved, why wouldn't you do it? *He owes me no loyalty*, I thought cynically. If he could give Joanna some consolation, some explanation for my distance, then why wouldn't he? I knew how much he cared for her, but it never occurred to me that he thought of me as anything resembling a friend.

I put the radio on and turned up the volume; I didn't want to think.

I was meeting two representatives from the studio in New York at the restaurant of a hotel in town. I had double-checked, and then triple-checked the information from their email last night and then again this morning.

I couldn't screw up this time.

I parked my car on the High Street. I was on time, and they were probably inside waiting for me. I grabbed my bag, but sat with it in my lap, biding my time. My method in life was usually to face everything with a wry smile. Why did this have to be any different? So I checked my lipstick in the overhead mirror, flattened my ever-wild hair and took a deep breath.

'Imogene,' a man said, waving for me as I entered the

seating area. I walked over to where the tall man with an eccentric handlebar moustache and a tall woman with short, red hair sat with coffee cups in front of them. 'Hi. I recognised you from the profile photo you sent us,' the man said, as he reached out his hand.

'You must be Mr Jepsen,' I said, shaking his hand.

'I am indeed, and this is Miss Carson,' he said, indicating the red-headed woman, with a wide hand gesture.

'It's nice to meet you, Imogene,' Miss Carson said, shaking my hand firmly. She was a younger woman, much younger than Mr Jepsen, who must have been approaching sixty. 'Have a seat.'

'I'm very grateful to you both for agreeing to meet me,' I said politely, taking a seat.

I glanced briefly at the other tables. All around me important-looking people appeared to be having important meetings, about what I'm sure were important things. Here I was, a misfit cellist in a blazer. Suddenly it wasn't so hard to smile, and I relaxed into the interview.

We discussed the New York studio's vision for contemporary classical music. We discussed my current employment, and I talked about my performance history. I could have talked for days.

'Imogene,' a familiar voice called out behind me.

Shit.

I turned reluctantly in my chair to witness the voice's owner approaching our table in a slow jaunt.

'Theo. What are you doing here?' I asked, forcing a smile that I had no doubt didn't reach my eyes.

He walked directly up to our table and leant a hand coolly on the back of my chair. He surveyed my interviewers. 'Hi, I'm Theo. A colleague of Imogene's,' he said, extending a hand to both of them.

Mr Jepsen smiled, closed lip, obviously puzzled by this

intrusion, but he shook Theo's hand nonetheless. Miss Carson appeared nonplussed. She shook his hand quickly as she nodded towards him, but her eyes glanced subtly in my direction.

'Theo, we're actually in the middle of a meeting,' I said candidly, my eyes concentrating hard on his face. He was more smartly dressed than usual, but his sly grin still looked the same.

'Oh, I'm so sorry for intruding,' he said feigning surprise and empathy.

'It was nice to meet you,' Miss Carson said dismissively, leaning forward and clasping her hands together on the table.

They wouldn't have noticed it, but I saw something twist in Theo's mind at this easy dismissal.

Double shit.

'Well, if I can be of any use in your assessment of our Imogene, here,' he said patting me on the shoulder, 'don't be afraid to contact me. You actually have my information on file. Theo Grisham. I applied for the position as well.' Miss Carson and Mr Jepsen exchanged a look. 'But Imogene here will do fantastically, I'm sure.'

Mr Jepsen laughed boisterously, unsure. 'Well we've definitely liked what we've heard so far.' He played with his curling moustache.

I smiled appreciatively. Under the table my fingernails dug into my palm nervously. *What is he going to say next?* I asked myself.

Theo smiled menacingly. 'She definitely is a talented musician. Too bad she could never actually take the job though,' he said solemnly, looking at his jacket as he picked at a bit of thread.

'Theo, shouldn't you…'

'I mean, it is understandable. If anything, staying and refusing the job offers you a keen insight into what type of person she really is. What kind of person would leave their family in their time of need? What kind of person would put their own ambitions ahead of their family's needs…' he drifted off. He shook his head, laughing sheepishly. My nails dug further into my palms.

'I am so sorry. I presume Imogene told you how she struggled with the passing of her parents. It kind of sent her off the rails; caused all kind of trouble with missing orchestra performances, and some days she just wouldn't show up to the studio. Almost getting arrested, going on week-long benders…'

'Theo, enough!' I snarled through gritted teeth. I stood up abruptly, causing the table to shake.

He smiled wickedly, before frowning at me mockingly. 'Calm down, Imogene. It was *lovely* to meet you both,' he nodded at the befuddled faces of my prospective employers.

Tears pricked my eyes as I stood there, too afraid to turn and meet their eyes. Simon was wrong. There was no point in trying. Who was I kidding?

You're damned if you do, and damned if you don't. At least, that's how it felt.

'I'm sorry, I…' I stuttered, turning around, looking down at the table. I just stood there.

'Well, why don't we just get on with the interview,' Mr Jepsen said gruffly, fiddling with his moustache once more before clasping his hands tightly together and resting them on the table. Miss Carson remained silent.

'I'm not sure…'

'Miss Payton, sit down,' Mr Jepsen said gratingly. I looked up, meeting his stare. 'You must learn to separate the different areas of your life if you wish to achieve success in this industry, or any industry for that matter! Now, shall we continue? Or will another *friend* of yours be joining us?'

I smiled bitterly. 'I'm sorry for wasting your time,' I said dryly, shaking my head. I turned and walked away. My jaw clamped shut as I bit back the tears and tried to keep the hysterical laugh from clawing up my throat and erupting into the open air.

'Miss Payton!' Mr Jepsen called after me.

There was no way I was turning around. I walked straight to my car, ignoring the obscure waves of faces that I passed on the pavement.

'Imogene?' Jason greeted me as I turned into the driveway. He was sitting on the front step, a book open in his lap. One of Mrs Vincent's butterfly cupcakes was on the step next to him. 'What's wrong?' he asked, his voice un-surprisingly mature-sounding as he closed his book.

I collapsed on the step next to him. I didn't have the energy to storm past him and lock myself away this time. So I sat on the step, facing my carelessly parked car.

'What book are you reading?' I asked, wiping my face with the back of my hand.

'*Gulliver's Travels*,' he said, holding it up to proudly show me the cover.

I nodded, 'It's a good book. Benson used to read it to us all the time.'

Jason's proud smile broadened as if that compilation of paper and ink had turned to pure gold at my statement.

I took my blazer off and placed it carelessly on the step behind me. I took a deep breath, and expelled my words as if they were full of poison. 'I had an interview today, and I blew it.'

'An interview for what?' he asked, curiously.

I paused brushing my hair back. 'A job that I wasn't even sure I wanted, but that I'm pretty sure I would have been perfect for.' I smiled pathetically.

'You don't know you blew it,' he said matter-of-factly, looking out at the driveway. 'You may think you know you did, but you actually have no idea what those people were thinking.'

You had to appreciate his optimism.

'Take you, for example. When I saw you were upset just then, I thought you would sooner drive your car into the house than talk to me about it.' He turned and grinned at me, raising his chin as he did so.

I frowned at him before grinning back.

'Here,' he said, picking up the cupcake and handing it to me.

'Are you sure?'

'I'm watching my weight,' he said, sucking in his stomach dramatically. I laughed, taking the cupcake and licking the icing. 'And you never know, you may get the job yet,' he said, raising his eyebrows and turning back to his book.

I took a bit of icing between my fingertips.

Their loss, my gain. Or would it be the other way around?

ELEVEN

Simon

'Hello?' I mumbled, groggily.

'Did I wake you up?' Leo said loudly, and a bit too enthusiastically.

I groaned, leaving the phone to rest haphazardly on the side of my face. 'What do you want?

'Charming. I'm outside. Open the front door.'

I ended the call and groaned again. Sluggishly I moved out of bed and down the hall to the front door. 'Hi,' I said opening the door to Leo's eager face. I blinked quickly against the harsh glare of the sun. The delightful weather didn't seem to mirror my early-morning mood.

'Coffee?' he asked, slapping me playfully on the back as he sauntered inside. I closed the door and turned around. He had already disappeared into the kitchen

'Come on in,' I mumbled sarcastically.

I slowly followed him into the kitchen. He was busy pouring coffee into two mugs, so I collapsed into a chair at the kitchen table. I inhaled the pleasant aroma of the steaming coffee. The clock above the oven said it was ten o'clock. It was my day off from my work experience, but apparently not my day off from babysitting Leo.

He put the mugs on the table and sat down. He looked so cheery that he was basically bouncing in his chair.

'Go on then, tell me what you're smiling about,' I asked, sipping my coffee.

He paused, as if creating a drum-roll out of the building silence. 'I asked Abbey on a date!' he said exuberantly.

My eyebrows shot up in shock, and I held my mug in mid-air. 'You did what?' I asked incredulously, lowering the mug to the safety of the table.

'OK, so I haven't exactly asked her yet, if you're being picky about it. But I'm going to, and that's what matters,' he said, rolling his eyes.

'If you say so,' I said, taking another sip to hide my smile, but it didn't work and he suddenly frowned at me.

'What? You don't think she'll say yes?' he asked, his enthusiasm now matched with a rising panic.

I shrugged, my smile growing. He groaned loudly.

'So when are you going to ask her?'

He frowned again, studying me. 'You're not surprised by this?'

I shrugged again, and rubbed my eyes. 'Not really, no. Joanna predicted this like five years ago, and I bet her that something would happen this summer, now you're both home from uni.'

'Huh,' he paused, thinking as he took a noisy slurp of his coffee. 'Do you think she's spoken to Joanna about us then?'

'No doubt about it,' I laughed. He smiled broadly at my bluntness.

'I might ask her tonight. You know, just bring it up casually.'

'What's tonight?'

'Charlie's thing,' Leo said. This time I was the one to groan loudly. 'Tell me what you really think about her,' Leo said mockingly. 'I thought you two had got closer this summer?'

I shook my head and gave him a brief and diluted version

of the other night's events, only wanting to make clear that I wasn't exactly her biggest fan at present.

'Well, I've already said I'm going, and I can't go without my other half, so I'm afraid you have no choice in the matter.' He raised his mug cheerily and winked at me.

'Does Abbey know that there will be three of us in the relationship?' I mumbled, finishing off my coffee. Leo laughed his hearty chuckle.

The rest of the day moved slowly. We moved from one room of the house to the next, as we sought entertainment. I went to take a shower at one point, and when I came back Leo was upside-down on the sofa eating Coco-Pops through a straw.

'Cambridge's finest, ladies and gentlemen,' I announced mockingly, as I threw myself onto the other sofa.

'Call it scientific curiosity,' he laughed, remaining upside-down.

Hours later, we had become so preoccupied by our attempt to be occupied, that we ended up running late. We only realised how late it was when my mum arrived home from work, tired and worn. She set her bags on the table, and when I asked her what she was doing this evening she pointed to a discouraging pile of folders. She never took a break. I kissed her on the cheek and told her not to work too hard. While Leo ran home to get changed, I heated up some frozen lasagne for us. Leo hurried back and as soon as he had gulfed down his food we headed out.

I was less than enthusiastic about the night ahead. The only plus was that Joanna was definitely going to be there, and together we could witness Leo's tragic attempt at playing Romeo.

'Hey!' Abbey greeted us, swinging open the door enthusiastically. She swung her arms around Leo and I, pulling us into a tight group hug. She released us and backed off slightly, a slight blush colouring her cheeks.

'Hey, guys.' Joanna's voice was much calmer than Abbey's but as she walked through the door her smile was immense. I pulled her into a tight hug. Leo threw his arms around both of us. 'Hello Leo!' Joanna laughed musically.

'When did you guys get here?' I asked, as they led us inside. The sounds of music and voices hit us like a wave as soon as we walked in.

'Charlie asked us to come over and get ready with her,' Abbey said cheerily.

Leo was looking all around him. People we knew from school were calling out to us as we walked down the hall to the kitchen. He seemed to share my confusion; there were way more people than I thought there would be. 'I thought she was just having a few people over,' he said as he waved his hand at someone who had just called his name.

'That was the plan,' Joanna laughed. 'But who knows with Charlie,' she added, raising her eyebrows at Abbey, who returned her look. Leo and I exchanged a confused look of our own.

'Where is our host?' I asked.

As if summoned by the very mention of the word, Charlie burst into the kitchen through a door that led out onto a stoned porch. Her house was like a maze, huge, and with an ostentatious feel to its architecture. Through the window I could see the vast garden from which she had just appeared, lit by small electric lights stuck into the grass.

'Guys!' she squealed. She bounced over to us, throwing her arms around Leo and I dramatically.

'Hey. We just got here,' Leo said, brushing his hair back as if to fix it.

'Awesome.' She eyed me up quickly as she pulled back. I didn't smile back at her.

Despite the awkward setting, Leo's attempts at implementing his plan kept me thoroughly entertained throughout the night. Every time he tried to talk to Abbey alone, a group of people ended up joining them, and he would throw me a look that made him look like a disgruntled puppy.

It was a pretty decent party. I hadn't seen a lot of the people there since going off to uni for the year. It was nice to hear what everyone was up to. I moved from room to room, from group to group, seeking to make the most of the night and try to enjoy myself. It was near the end of the night when I decided I needed a bit of air.

'Thought I'd find you out here,' Joanna said, walking over the pebbled path to where I sat on a randomly placed bench, halfway between the house and the end of the garden.

The bench was facing away from the house, so that the intertwining noise of the blaring music and rising voices hit our backs and didn't claim the attention of our ears. The garden sloped downwards slightly, so that over the hedge-row lights were spotted like urban stars. Joanna collapsed tiredly onto the bench next to me, leaning some of her weight on me as she rested against my side.

'Seems I can't hack the pace any more. But apparently neither can you, so I don't mind too much,' I laughed, looking down at her as she rested her head on my shoulder.

She raised her head to grin at me, shoving my arm playfully. She pushed back her hair and sighed. 'Sometimes I think I'm an old woman trapped in a younger body. Jason's probably curled up in bed with a book right now, and as tragic as I sound, I am immensely jealous of him.' She laughed gently, her eyes twinkling in the glow of the garden lamps. She put her drink down on the path.

'Charlie seems to be having a great time though,' she said, raising her eyebrows suggestively.

'Yay,' I said, my monotone reeking of sarcasm.

'What is going on with you two lately? One minute I hear

you're having lovey-dovey coffee dates and the next minute you apparently hate each other.'

A heavy frown formed on my face as I guffawed incredulously. 'We have never, and will never, go on lovey-dovey dates, but I don't hate her,' I said bluntly.

Something itched my brain. I didn't like the easy assumption that Joanna had made. But I think what really didn't sit well with me was the carefree way in which she seemed to make it. Did she care?

'I know she isn't the easiest of people, but she's a good friend,' Joanna added, brushing off my annoyance.

I simply scoffed, and Joanna frowned back at me, mirroring my annoyance, but for a different reason.

'Guys!' A unified yell came from behind us. Leo, Abbey and Charlie came running over to us, pausing only when they stood right in front of us. Leo sat clumsily on the grass and Abbey sat next to Joanna, a grin and a gentle blush painting her face with enjoyment. Charlie stood directly in front of us next to where Leo sat. She folded her arms and surveyed us.

'You can't seem to stay away from the Payton girls, can you, Simon?' she asked, a menacing grin curling her lips up at either side.

'What are you talking about, Charlie?' Joanna asked calmly, looking up at her benevolently, as if she were an adult bemusing a child.

'Well that's if you count Imogene as a Payton girl,' she added.

Joanna's face fell. 'What?' she questioned again, no longer smiling.

'Sorry,' Charlie said, innocently, 'I thought he would have told you. Simon played the knight in shining armour the other night. Imogene was going completely ballistic…'

'Enough, Charlie,' I said, rolling my eyes, before turning

my attention to Joanna. 'Imogene was upset at a party the other night, so I made sure she got home OK.'

'Yeah. He was really kind to her, especially considering what nasty things she was saying about all of you...' Charlie's voice tailed off.

Joanna's face had become blank, forming a mask that I recognised well but could never make out. Leo and Abbey remained as still as they possibly could. Their eyes looked between the three characters acting in the show before them.

'That's not true, Charlie. But you have made a habit of telling lies, so why should I be surprised?' I said, my temper rising.

Joanna pushed herself off of the seat, her hand brushing subtly, but familiarly, up and down her scarred arm.

'Thank you for making sure she got home OK,' she said to me, her eyes piercing mine. 'I'm sure she appreciated his help,' she said, this time looking directly at Charlie, her voice dry and each word heavy with the deliberateness with which it was said. 'And yes, I would count Imogene as a Payton girl.'

Charlie's smirk disappeared, replaced by clear embarrassment.

'Let's go back inside. It's getting cold.'

Abbey stood up, and took Joanna's hand before following her inside. Leo slapped me on the shoulder as I walked alongside him back to the house. I didn't look back to see if Charlie followed.

It wasn't long after we had gone back inside that I noticed Joanna slip on her jacket, whisper something to Abbey, and head towards the front door. I followed her outside, pushing past people as I moved across the room and back out into the crisp night air.

'I'm going home, Simon,' Joanna said, as she walked down the steps of the front porch. She paused when her feet met the gravel of the driveway, turning to look at me. 'I'm tired, so I'm going home. It's as simple as that,' she laughed, each note ringing with an exhaustion that extended further than that of physicality.

I stood in front of her. She was upset, but I couldn't find the words to make it all OK.

'Why didn't you just tell me you helped Imogene? Why does everything have to become some big secret?' she asked, throwing her hands up with exasperation. 'By keeping things secret you turn things into something that they're not. You… you let people like Charlie think they have the right to have an opinion on things that have nothing to do with them.'

I couldn't help but laugh at the absurdity of it all. She crossed her arms, and raised her eyebrows at me.

'That's exactly it, though! I didn't tell you because Imogene asked me not to. I didn't tell you because, frankly' – I knew I was going to regret this – 'not everything needs to involve you, Joanna.'

The hurt was plain on her face, and the scarce light escaping the house illuminated the tears forming in her eyes.

'But it is your concern? Since when does my sister ask *you* for help?' She threw her hands up to her hair, shaking her head. 'You act like I'm in the wrong, like I'm intruding into business not of my concern. But I am so tired of you treating me like a china doll when all I'm doing is trying to help.'

'Is that so different from what you do?'

'What are you talking about? This is *my* family we're talking about.'

'It's more than that, you know it is.' I paused, putting my hands on my hips as I breathed deeply. If she didn't want me to protect her, than I wouldn't sugar-coat it. 'You focus so much on trying to make everyone else happy, on trying to fix everything else around you, and you only end up hurting yourself even more. Imogene has every right to her own secrets, Joanna. Just like you have every right to yell and scream and cry, rather than trying to paint a smile on everyone else's faces.'

My voice had dropped to a solemn whisper, and without meaning to we had moved closer to each other, now only inches away. Her face appeared to glisten as angry tears drifted down her cheeks, marking her skin.

'Sometimes you have to let people fight their own battles,' I finally sighed.

It wasn't my secret to tell; it was Imogene's. In an effort to protect Joanna I felt that I was pushing her away. Yet deep down I knew I meant every word. Nothing I said was a lie.

A door slammed behind us. I turned around and a couple of people came stumbling down the porch, chattering loudly. I turned back to Joanna, but she was already walking away.

TWELVE

Joanna

I got home just as it started to rain. I heard the drops beating gently against the wood of the door as I stood with my back to it. I swallowed as a lump formed in my throat, and I felt a shiver pass through me.

I had decided to walk home rather than getting a taxi or calling someone to pick me up. At first I just didn't want anyone to see me angry, and then I just wanted the time to think. There's little worse than being angry and not knowing entirely what it is you're angry about.

I had no idea what time it was, but I knew it was late as the house was eerily still. All of the downstairs lights were off, so I stood there, illuminated only by the porch light shining in through the windows.

I sank to the floor of the hallway, releasing a sigh. Suddenly I just wanted to curl up into a ball and go to sleep right there by the front door. *That would be an interesting sight for Katrina to witness in the morning*, I thought.

'Hey,' I whispered, as Jerry pattered slowly over to me. 'What are you doing down here?' I wondered aloud. He usually slept up in Jason's room.

He sat down in front of me, panting with his tongue lolling to the side. I ran my hands through his fur, moving them up and down his back. His fur was so soft, it felt nice under my cold hands.

'I couldn't sleep,' Jason said, emerging from the kitchen.

I jolted back, caught off-guard, and hit my head on the door behind me. 'Ow,' I moaned.

Jason snorted with laughter, the sound breaking the quiet that had been hanging over the house.

I rubbed the back of my head. Jerry lay down lazily in front of me. Jason walked over and sat next to me on the floor, crossing his legs underneath him.

'You know your pyjamas make you look like an old man,' I told him.

'You know you look like Bridget Jones before she gets herself together and marries Darcy,' he retorted, completely straight-faced.

Laughter erupted from my mouth, completely distracting me from the gentle throbbing at the back of my head. Jason shush'd me, telling me that I would wake up the whole house. His grin suddenly made him look so much younger.

'Go on then, tell me what happened,' he said, turning his head to look at me expectantly. 'I seem to be doing a fair bit of comforting these days.'

'What are you talking about?'

'Imogene was upset earlier as well,' he shrugged. 'She had an interview or something and she didn't think it went well.'

'Do you know what it was an interview for?' I asked.

'She didn't say,' he shrugged, looking at Jerry who had rolled onto his side.

'Of course,' I said quietly, expelling the words bitterly.

Jason just frowned at me, before raising his eyebrows for me to continue.

'Simon told me today that he had helped her out the other night.' I sighed. 'Imogene's been pushing back at me more than usual lately. At first I thought it was because the

90

anniversary was coming up. But then Simon told me that she had turned to him for help.'

Silence fell once more around us.

'Now I hear she's confided in you as well,' I added, a quiet, bitter laugh escaping my lips. I hesitated. 'There was something else as well; something Charlie said. She made some snide remark about Imogene not really being a part of the family. Then Simon piled on by going on about how it was none of my business. He kept going on, talking about things he had no right to have an opinion on.'

'Are you sure he wasn't just trying to help? It's not like you guys to fight,' Jason whispered.

'Probably,' I admitted, sighing as I rubbed my eyes tiredly. 'I don't know.' I sighed again.

We sat in silence for a bit. I let my eyes roam around the darkened house, and Jason extended his hand out to Jerry who shuffled himself over to rest his head on Jason's lap.

'You need to tell him how you really feel.'

'What?' I asked the heat rushing to my face as my head spun around.

'I don't know! It's what they're always saying in those stupid movies Katrina watches,' he said quickly, holding his hands up in self-defence. 'Thought I'd give it ago,' he added as he shrugged with a subtle smile.

I punched him lightly on the arm, shaking my head. I blinked my eyes slowly as tiredness and intoxication made the dark hall spin gently. I sighed and tried to focus my mind.

'In all seriousness though, Joanna,' he said, suddenly straight-faced, looking at me directly, 'don't be mad at Simon. I mean, I'm not going to lie, I'm not entirely sure what you're angry at, but I'm sure whatever it was he was just trying to help.'

I swallowed and leant my head back against the cold wood of the door. I brushed my jacket sleeve up, my scars revealing themselves to the illumination of the porch light shining in through the windows above us. I let my finger tips trace mindlessly up and down my arms as my gaze found a point of far-off focus.

'It's OK,' I said quietly.

Jason snorted loudly. 'OK, cool. You definitely convinced me.' He snorted again, this time apparently at his own sarcasm.

I rolled my eyes.

'Why don't we do something tomorrow? All four of us?' he said, trying to layer a tone of casualness on top of his obvious excitement at the possibility.

I didn't say anything, but instead let the incredulous expression on my face speak for itself.

'What? It might be nice, you never know. It might be fun,' he laughed.

He was so hard to say no to. I told him if Katrina and Imogene were up for it, then why not?

After I said goodnight to Jason we departed to our separate rooms, Jerry padding loyally after his little master. When I got to my room I threw my bag to one side and slung my jacket carelessly over my desk chair. Slipping off my boots I climbed into bed, wrapping my duvet comfortably around myself as I let the melodic sound of raindrops on glass lull me to sleep.

Images of Simon filled my night-bound subconscious, breaking out like paint being thrown onto a blank canvas. Charlie's harsh words struck at me like fire biting my fingertips, but she wasn't the only one haunting my slumber. My reflection, bearing down on me from a haunting mirror, threw words at me that cut worse than Charlie's ever could. The fire bit further up my left arm. However, falling in line with the confusion that dreams often bring, the scene quickly changed. I woke feeling better than I had when I went to sleep. And I had a brilliant idea.

'So I hear Jason's holding us captive this afternoon,' Katrina said as I joined her in the living room.

She was reclining horizontally on one of the sofas, her mug resting precariously on the arm of a chair while she focused on the magazine she held in her hand.

'So I heard,' I replied, leaping onto the other sofa. 'What's he got in store for us?'

'He said something about not wanting to scare Imogene away, so he thought he'd keep it simple with a movie marathon,' Katrina said, raising her eyebrows at me jovially. 'I can't even remember the last time we were all in the same room together.'

I gave her a tongue-in-cheek smile in response. 'Is he upstairs?'

'Nope. He went over to Mrs Vincent's for a bit.'

I rearranged myself into a sitting position, with my knees together, my hands clasped as I leant forward on my elbows.

'Katrina…' I began, trailing off my sentence to catch her attention.

It worked. She lowered her magazine to eye me curiously.

'I am an adult, so I'm telling you this just because I wanted to get your opinion, you know, being the considerate niece that I am.'

She snorted loudly, obviously not buying my sincerity.

I didn't get to start my discussion of the idea I had the previous night, as the doorbell rang loudly, breaking my flow.

I held up a finger. 'Stay there,' I instructed.

She nodded obediently. 'I'm very curious, Miss Payton,' she called.

I walked towards the front door as the bell sounded again, ringing out loudly with impatience.

'Coming!' I called, raising my voice to be heard over the strident bell.

I swung open the door.

'You and Simon are eloping and running away to join the circus!' Katrina yelled out, just as I opened the door to the man himself.

The corners of his mouth turned up gently. 'Planning a trip I don't know about?' he said casually, mock confusion furrowing his brow momentarily.

'Who is it?' Katrina shouted, completely oblivious.

'The man I'm running away to join the circus with!' I yelled back.

'Whoops,' I heard her say quietly, followed by a barely audible chuckle.

'What's up?' I said to Simon brusquely, turning my attention back to him. He was standing on the doormat with his hands in his pockets. His hair stuck up unevenly, raindrops dripping onto the shoulders of his jacket. I hadn't even known it was raining.

'Can we talk, please?'

I felt the heat rush up to my cheeks. I felt the corners of my mouth turn up, threatening to break my angry facade.

'What?' he asked, smiling confusedly.

'I don't think you've ever spoken to me so formally,' I said honestly. 'Why don't we go upstairs?'

He followed me up to my room, waving to Katrina as we passed the lounge. She remained reclined on the sofa, simply raising her mug to us as we passed.

'I don't have a lot of time. Jason's planned an evening for us,' I said dismissively as we entered my room. I sat on the bed, and he sat on the desk chair, pulling it around to face me.

'I...' Simon began. He was interrupted by Jason bursting into the room, a smile stretching across his face.

'Simon. Hi,' he said, trying to recover a sense of casualness. 'Are you free tonight?'

'Jason...' I began to protest, but again I was interrupted by the youngest member of my never-so-subtle family.

'We're having a movie night and Katrina's made some food. Are you free? Brilliant! I'll see you later then,' he said without waiting for a response. He swept out of the room after saluting his farewell. I heard him running down the stairs as my bedroom door swung shut.

'Well, it seems like I'm not going anywhere, so we have all the time in the world,' Simon said drolly. 'Oh come on, Joanna. You can't stay angry at me forever. Yell at me, say whatever you want to say.'

I sighed as I looked from him to my hands, intertwined in my lap.

'It's fine. I'm not angry.' I sighed, getting up from the bed. I moved to the foot of my bed, looking at all of the photos and posters I had covered the walls with. I could feel his eyes watching me.

'Seriously?' he scoffed. 'You left the party in tears, and you're not angry at me in the slightest?'

I turned to face him, frustration rising within me. 'No. I'm not angry. In fact,' I threw my hands up mockingly, 'I've never been happier! But do you know what I would really love? What would make me even happier than I already am? If you would stop trying to provoke me.'

I paused, running my hands through my hair. I spun around, turning full circle, coming back to face him. He remained sitting in the chair, his blank expression revealing nothing.

'What was it you said?' I continued, my voice heavily sarcastic. 'Oh yeah, "Sometimes you have to let other people fight their own battles". So why is any of this any of *your* concern?' I hadn't realised how loud my voice had grown until I was met with the uncomfortable silence that followed my outburst.

Angry tears were building in my eyes, threatening to ruin my attempt at appearing tenacious. I let out a hearty sigh that broke through the silence. Simon's eyes had not escaped mine, but he now stood up.

'Didn't it ever cross your mind that I don't want to be angry,' I said, almost whispering.

My right hand found my left arm, the familiarity of this comforting act now coupled with the thrilling possibility of what I hoped to do. I wondered what Simon would think of my plan?

He stepped forward and took my left hand. I let my right hand fall to my side as he held my scarred hand in his.

'You're right. I'm sorry,' he said clearly, his voice carrying a level of composure. 'I was being hypocritical and I'm sorry. I was trying to stop you from helping, when that was all I was trying to do myself.'

I let my left hand fall from his.

'I just...' Simon began, but the rest of the words seemed to fly away. He looked as if the words were physically caught in his throat. He looked at me, his eager eyes searching mine, as if he wanted me to figure out what he was trying to say without him having to say it.

'What?'

Then Jason called up to us, telling us to come down stairs.

'Jason told me to fetch you two,' Imogene said, pushing the door open with the palm of her hand. Her face seemed to harden when she saw Simon. She pushed her hair back and folded her arms, waiting.

She looked slowly back and forth between Simon and I, before rolling her eyes and going back out of the room. I looked back at Simon and then quickly followed Imogene. I was halfway down the stairs before I heard him shut my door and follow us.

Despite the awkwardness, Simon stayed until late that night. Jason seemed to be enjoying every minute of us all being in the same room. Imogene didn't have a whole lot to say, as usual, and threw out a few snide remarks, but overall she seemed to enjoy the night too. That was the weirdest part.

THIRTEEN

Imogene

'Hello?' I mumbled, barely audible as morning grogginess muffled my voice.

'Hello? Imogene, it's Miss Carson here,' she said, her voice ringing clear with a tone of formality.

I shot up in my bed, frowning as I looked around my still darkened room. Why was she calling me?

'Um, hi,' I replied, clearing my throat.

'As I'm sure you can guess, I am calling you in relation to your interview,' she continued.

I sighed internally, a resigned smile resting itself on my face. 'I apologise again...'

'I know it is short notice,' she persisted, ignoring my interruption completely, 'but if you are available later on today I was wondering if you would be able to meet me for an audition. I have been able to procure a studio room for this afternoon. The other day, I feel, I didn't get a chance to fully assess the talent you have to offer us. So I would like to offer you the chance to perform two pieces for myself and Mr Jepsen.'

I was taken aback.

'Hello? Miss Payton?' she asked, in response to my dumbfounded silence.

'Yes. Sorry. I'm still here,' I stammered. My mind was

spinning. I couldn't decipher my own thoughts and feelings enough to form a coherent reply.

I hadn't expected this; part of me didn't want it. Nonetheless I heard myself say what I thought I should, 'Yes. Yes, I'll… I'll be there.'

'Great,' she said, expelling the words as if relieved. She was obviously going out on a limb by giving me a second chance. She appeared to compose herself, the rest of her words hitting the phone line in a crisp, blunt manner. 'I will email you the address, and will expect you at two o'clock. We will see you then.'

'OK,' was all I could manage in terms of farewell. She hung up on her end, but I sat and listened to the dial tone, stunned. 'OK.'

I checked the time on my phone. I had six hours. I fell back onto my pillows.

Only now that I had been given the grace of a second chance could I fully process my feelings towards tanking the previous interview. Part of me had seen it as a way out. I had failed, but through that failure I had succeeded in not having to face an even greater fear.

But now I had the chance to perform. Goodness knows what Miss Carson was thinking. I couldn't help but smile; if I was her, I definitely wouldn't want to employ me.

I couldn't fall back to sleep, so I clambered out of bed. I spent the rest of the morning analysing possible pieces I could perform, before settling on one piece that I had performed publicly last year, and so knew was a safe choice. The second piece I decided to run with was one which I had recently composed myself. I decided that if I was going to do it, then what was the point in holding anything back?

I let the sorrowful melodies of Sylvain Chauveau and Elinor Frey fill my room. I shut out all other distractions and filled my ears with the soulful sound of the bitter-sweet instrument.

I had tried and failed at a lot of instruments before I settled on the cello. I had told Vera I was crap at music, but she refused to believe me, even though she only had to listen to my attempt at playing the flute to see the truth in my complaints. She started paying for me to get cello lessons at school. If anything, I was at least consistent, as I complained and complained. But soon enough I started to believe her; to believe that I was actually decent at something. I wasn't academic like Joanna, and I wasn't sporty, but I found my metier in an instrument of elegant sorrow.

'Aren't you working today?'

My head spun around, causing my neck to crick sharply. 'Jason, I told you not to sneak up on me like that,' I rebuked him.

'I did knock,' he replied resolutely, folding his arms across his chest.

'What do you want?' I asked, rising from my desk chair to put my cello in its case. It was almost time to leave. I slammed my laptop shut, and gathered all the paper that was strewn like a musical ocean around my room.

'Aren't you working today?' he repeated, walking further into the room to lean on the foot of my bed.

'No. Kind of.'

He scoffed. 'What does that mean?'

I paused, sighing as I turned to look at him, running my hands through my hair trying to flatten it. 'You know that interview I was telling you about a while ago? Well, they're giving me another chance. I have to go and audition for them in town at two o'clock.'

'That's great!' he said, appearing genuinely excited.

I smiled, wishing I shared his pure excitement.

'Can I come?' he asked.

I glowered at him before quickly taking a look at myself in the mirror. I was dressed simply in a pair of dark denim jeans, a plain white shirt and my black blazer. I ran my hands through my hair again, and grabbed my red lipstick from my chest of drawers.

He continued with his plea. 'Everyone's busy today, and I'm bored. Joanna's working at Abbey's restaurant today, and Katrina's throwing paint at a canvas in the garden. I won't be annoying, I promise!' he persisted. 'And besides, with my adorable face by your side they'll definitely give you the job!' He held his hands under his chin like a human frame, and batted his eyelashes dramatically.

'You're going to be just as bored if you come. You'll probably have to stay in the car…'

He shrugged and continued to smile broadly at me. He folded his arms again and looked at me expectantly.

I let out a moan. 'Fine. We leave in ten minutes.'

He nodded contently, trying not to look to smug.

It didn't take us long to get there. I had printed out directions from the email Miss Carson had sent me.

I didn't recognise the name of the studio rooms, which I thought was unusual.

'This looks like the scene of a murder,' was Jason's mature remark upon our driving into the parking lot.

I didn't disagree with him. The building was a massive, grey, concrete mass. Obviously, some sort of factory had been reconstructed into studios. We went through the glass double doors at the front of the building. Inside, opposite the doors, was a sign listing the various rooms, marked by number.

'It's like the Tardis,' Jason whispered, as I tried to decipher the sign whilst leaning on my heavy cello case.

The building appeared even bigger from within. Unlike its bland, industrial exterior, inside it was surprisingly modern. A staircase to the left of the doors ascended perilously, and in every direction wood-panelled doors seemed to lead to unknown rooms.

'OK, I think the room we have to go to is on the third floor,' I told him, lifting the case and proceeding up the stairs.

Jason followed quietly behind me. He probably thought that the quieter he was, the less likely I was to exile him to the confines of the car.

In one of the rooms we passed, young children were immersed in a ballet lesson. In another room some women were sweating it out in a pilates session. As we moved further up the swirling staircase, most of the rooms seemed to be occupied, and yet the staircase remained a tunnel of silence.

We stopped on the landing of the third floor, then proceeding through a door to our left we found our sought-for room at the end of a short corridor.

'OK,' I grimaced as we paused outside the door. I looked down at Jason, undecided as to what to do with him.

'Silent and cute. Don't worry, I've got this,' he said, rubbing his hands together, as if reading my mind.

Turning back to the door I nodded in silent affirmation before slowly opening it.

Walking into the room I immediately saw Miss Carson and Mr Jepsen sitting on wooden chairs at the far side of the room. The room was slightly bigger than any of the other ones we had seen, with mirrors panelling most of the four walls, giving the room a feeling of endlessness. Behind Miss Carson and Mr Jepsen was a giant window, framed by heavy velvet curtains. A few more chairs sat in the corner of the room, in the natural light coming in from the window. Opposite my interviewers, however, was a single, straight-backed, wooden chair.

I walked tentatively into the room. Mr Jepsen remained sitting down, a shrewd look carved on his face. Miss Carson, however, walked over to me.

'Miss Payton, I'm glad you could make it,' she said levelly, extending her hand. I shook it firmly, smiling and nodding.

'Who is this?' she asked, eyeing Jason who was standing silent to my left, taking in the room.

'I'm her brother, Jason,' he said, introducing himself. He extended his hand out as he had watched her do, and Miss Carson shook it, amusement twinkling her eyes. She looked to me for an explanation. 'Imogene's babysitting me and she thought it would be useful for me to accompany her today. We hope that's OK?' he asked.

I had to try my hardest not to laugh. Mr Jepsen sat silently, eyeing us with utter disinterest. This meeting obviously hadn't been his idea. This only made me want to laugh more.

'Of course it is,' Miss Carson agreed. 'Why don't you go sit over there,' she said, indicating the chairs off to the side. 'Shall we begin?'

Jason walked off, and sat down with his hands folded in his lap. Walking over to the isolated chair in the centre of the room, I placed my cello case on the floor. Removing my blazer, I placed it over the back of the chair. I glanced up as Miss Carson took her seat again.

'Good afternoon, Mr Jepsen,' I said as politely as I could manage, nodding in his direction now that I stood in front of him.

He huffed in response, and I thought I saw Miss Carson's face tighten.

I pushed my tongue against the roof of my mouth as I tried to maintain my composure. *Just do it*, I thought.

So I did. I played, and I let that speak for itself.

I blocked out everything and everyone. My fingers danced along the strings, and I felt the bow caress the strings in a dance controlled by instinct. Having memorised the pieces I didn't need to look at sheet music, and so focused on the instrument. I closed my eyes as I felt the melody flow through my ears and into my veins. I let the melancholy of the music release the affliction I had been facing up until that moment.

I finished playing the first piece. Miss Carson nodded. Jason started clapping until he realised he was the only one. He pressed his lips together, embarrassed. I winked at him, hoping to show my appreciation.

I introduced the second piece. I hadn't yet given it a name, and so I gave a quick description of my influences, inspirations and a brief sketch of the emotion behind the piece.

'Proceed,' was all Mr Jepsen said, speaking brusquely as he fiddled with his elaborate moustache.

I exhaled slowly, and using the confidence which the execution of the first piece had given me, I played. I bared my soul through the originality of my piece.

Before I knew it, it was over.

Miss Carson clapped her hands together when I finished. She told me they had a lot to discuss but would contact me within the week.

I placed the cello back in its case. I put my blazer back on, the fit feeling especially tight after the free-flowing movement my arms had just experienced.

That was it. I shook their hands and Jason and I were on our way.

'Well, that went well,' Jason said optimistically, as we walked out to the car.

My stomach was still flipping nervously, proving I obviously didn't share his optimism. I didn't talk much as we drove home. My insides were a swirling pit of mixed emotions. Jason eventually gave up trying to make conversation and turned the radio up, blaring the music as we made the short journey home.

When we got to the house, I went to pull into the drive but there was already another car parked alongside Katrina's. It was a beaten-up red Volvo. I recognised the car.

What is he doing here? I thought.

'Who's that?' Jason voiced, straining his neck to catch

a glimpse of the driver as the car began backing out of the driveway.

I reversed slightly to give him room, and so as he spun back our cars ended up facing each other. He paused slightly, a dark grin stretching across his features. I hadn't spoken to Theo in weeks, and now he was pulling out of my driveway. What confused me more was that seeing me didn't seem to have been the purpose of the visit. He drove on past me, offering me nothing more than a smirk and a casual wave of his hand.

I parked the car. Jason asked repeatedly who he was, asking if he was a friend of mine. I ignored him, getting out of the car and slamming the door behind me. I didn't bother locking the doors but walked on and into the house.

I heard Jerry barking in the garden, but I found Joanna sitting at the dining room table. Her face was sullen, and the look of betrayal in her eyes was anything but subtle. She still wore her white shirt and black trousers from work.

'Theo popped by,' she began, choosing to look at her tightly clasped hands instead of me.

Jason had followed me inside and stood in the doorway, rolling back and forth on his heels, unsure.

'We saw him,' I said bluntly, watching her carefully. 'Was he asking for me?'

'I told him you weren't here. He told me to tell you good luck. He says he hopes you have a *great* time in New York.'

'You're going to New York?' Jason asked, smiling confusedly.

'Didn't she tell you, Jason?' she asked, pushing her hands against the table as she stood up. Exasperation and despondency seemed to drag her posture closer to the floor. 'Why didn't you just tell us?' she asked quietly, looking up at me slowly.

'It's none of your business,' I said, almost in a whisper.

I kicked myself internally.

She threw her hands up to her head, a bitter and slightly

104

hysterical laugh escaping her lips. 'You're moving halfway across the world in a month and you honestly thought it was *none of our business!*' she yelled at me.

'You're moving to New York?' Jason whispered behind me.

I turned to face him, but I couldn't seem to say anything. I didn't know what to say. I just kept looking back and forth between them. My jaw clamped shut as my bewilderment grew.

'I'm sorry,' I said bluntly, pathetically.

Joanna spun around and seemed to grow more hysterical, angry tears now running freely down her face.

'I don't have to deal with this,' I said quietly, swallowing the lump that had grown in my throat. I began to walk out of the room, but Joanna stopped me.

'Don't walk away from us!' she yelled, 'Don't you dare walk away,' she said quieter. 'Why didn't you just tell us? Why do you never just talk to us?'

I didn't respond, but pushed my hair back and sighed.

She moved over to where I stood close to the door. 'Fine!' she said, the tears flowing freely now. 'Go! Leave! Just leave and pretend that you don't care, because that's all you seem able to do!'

As she spoke she shoved my shoulders. I didn't move and so she tried to make me. She pushed me again, harder this time. Then she just started hitting me, crying, throwing her fists against my shoulders and torso. The hits weren't hard and I deflected most of them.

I managed to catch her arms. Fighting against her balled-up fists I pulled her towards me. I closed my arms around her, hugging her tightly. She cried more and tried to push away from me before I felt her go limp in my arms as she gave in.

'It's OK,' I said, quietly trying to soothe her.

She calmed, her crying easing, and her breathing slowing.

I let go of her. She pushed the wet strands of hair behind her ears. Sighing, she sat on the floor, collapsing with her back against the kitchen island.

'It's not OK,' she whispered. 'I'm sorry,' she said, her voice soft and regretful.

I sat next to her on the floor, resting my head back and placing my hands against the cool tiles on the floor.

'You're right. It's not OK,' I said flatly.

She turned to look at me, and in that brief moment I think more understanding flowed between us than it had in years.

'You're both insane. Can we please go back to the fact that you're moving?' Jason said, throwing his hands up in the air as if we had all lost our minds.

'Sit down,' I told him.

He frowned stubbornly at me before following suit and sitting on the floor in front of us, his legs crossed, leaning his head in his hands as he rested his elbows on his thighs.

It wasn't OK. Nothing was OK. But I had secured a sense of strength in the past six hours that I hadn't felt in a long time. So I told them everything.

I explained what the interview had been for, I told them how I had struggled with whether or not I should go for it, that I was still struggling over the decision. I explained to them just how not OK I really was. Joanna's outburst had made me realise I had to. It was as if something inside me had suddenly clicked; I didn't want her to break too.

I had the same feeling as on the night I had spoken to Simon. I felt a mixture of guilt, anger, grief... but most significantly I felt relief.

They asked me questions and I answered them as best I could. We talked for what felt like hours. By the time we finished, and were sitting in an aftermath of silence, it was getting dark outside.

Joanna was the one who broke the silence. She started chuckling. She shook her head in hilarious despair and rubbed her eyes.

'I told Ben my family was weird,' Jason said, shaking his head also.

Joanna snorted with laughter and I smiled.

'At least we're not boring,' Joanna added. But then her smile faded and she looked at me dejectedly. 'I'm sorry you've been going through all of that. I should have known.' She hung her head slightly, her shoulders drooped.

'No,' I sighed, before staring at her sternly. 'I'm sorry. I had no right to act like I did after… I've been so selfish,' I whispered.

The front door slammed, and Katrina wandered in, carrying plastic bags and a large canvas. She paused when she got to the kitchen doorway. She lowered the canvas to the floor as she surveyed the three of us sitting on the kitchen floor. My cello and handbag were discarded by the doorway, along with Jason's bag. Joanna was still in her work clothes and her face was red and puffy with obvious tear lines.

Katrina raised her eyebrows before asking, 'Is everything OK…?' drawing out the last word.

'I'm not sure I'd go as far as that,' Jason said drolly, raising his eyebrows back.

Joanna rested her head on my shoulder.

FOURTEEN

Simon, Fourteen Years Ago

'What am I meant to do?' my mum wept. She was sitting at the table, burying her face in her hands.

I knew why she was crying. I didn't want her to cry.

'I just never thought he would actually leave,' she continued, a tragic sigh stifling her sobs.

I looked up from where I was playing on the floor in the lounge. Discarded pieces of Lego surrounded me where I sat with my legs crossed.

Mrs Vincent looked over at me from where she sat next to my mum. She held my gaze until I eventually looked back to the floor.

'Allana, listen to me,' she said sternly. 'What's done is done,' she continued, lowering her voice significantly, obviously not intending for me to hear.

It had been a couple of days since I had seen my dad. I didn't really understand why I hadn't seen him. Mum just kept telling me he was working hard.

Mrs Vincent continued to talk quietly to Mum. She held my mum's hand, while my mum covered her face with the other. Mum let her hand fall to the table, and with a look to concern any five-year-old, she gazed at me. The tears streamed slowly down her face.

I didn't want her to cry.

'I know, I know,' she said, her voice much louder than Mrs Vincent's had been. She released a massive sigh, which seemed to amplify the atmospheric silence.

'You have a good job, you work hard, and make enough to get by. Plus you have good friends and a son that is braver and smarter than you might think,' Mrs Vincent said, patting mum's hands gently, while she spoke with a stern resilience.

My mum nodded, staring at the older woman who sat opposite her.

'That reminds me, I need to call work back,' she said, nodding again as she rose from the table. 'Mummy, will be back in a minute Simon,' she called to me, although the very acknowledgement of my presence appeared to make her well up even more.

I silently watched her walk into the other room.

Mrs Vincent walked across the room and sat on the sofa, looking down at me where I played. I threw the pieces I had in my hand at the ground; I didn't want to play anymore.

'Have you finished playing?' she asked me, clasping her hands together in her lap.

Her grey hair fell across her shoulder in the same braid that she always wore it in.

I shrugged. 'Is Dad still at work?'

She watched me pensively. 'No.' She paused before continuing. 'Your dad has decided that his adventure is to take place elsewhere.'

'What adventure?'

'His *adventure*, Simon. You see, you and I are on an adventure right now.'

I scrunched up my face at her with immature petulance. 'No we're not.'

She smiled at me with a wry smile. 'Of course we are. Every day is an adventure, Simon.'

I stared at her, still unconvinced, and surprisingly unamused considering my young age.

She sighed and seemed to hum to herself as she thought. 'Do you like to read?'

I nodded.

'Well, we are just like the characters in the books you read. Not every day of the characters' lives is filled with treasure hunts, rescue missions and travels to magical lands, but every day and every page makes up the adventure of their lives. Every single thing that happens to them is part of the adventure; every word counts, everyone they meet matters. So, just because your dad isn't here anymore, doesn't mean that you and your mother's adventures have to end. This is simply a chapter of the book. Your adventure continues. He is an important character, indeed he is, but you, Simon, are the hero of your own story.'

I tipped my head to the side, trying to understand what she meant. I no longer frowned, but my expression remained a picture of puzzlement.

She laughed, a quiet and hearty chuckle.

'You'll understand what I mean, one day.'

And I did.

FIFTEEN

Jason, Three Weeks before the Anniversary

Joanna and Imogene had been spending a lot more time together the past few weeks. Imogene had been joining us for meals, and Joanna hadn't been making a poignant effort to avoid Imogene. As expected, things were a bit weird after Joanna's outburst and the conversation that followed.

I was more shocked than anything. Obviously I see everything differently. I was so much younger when it happened; I've grown up with the ways things are being the norm. It took me a while to even understand what it meant when people kept saying that Imogene was adopted. She had always been around in my life, a part of my family, and so I didn't think anything of it.

I sometimes think that Katrina and Joanna interpret my lack of understanding as naivety. Imogene even said that was one of the reasons why she had never told me everything that was going on, because I was still so young. I think that's where I differ most from my sisters and my aunt; they see the fact that I'm a child as a signature of naivety. But I see it as the reason why I'm able to understand everything going on with us. I would much rather be a wallflower than a cactus in the heat of the desert.

I didn't like the idea of Imogene moving away. America was very far away, after all, and I doubted we would be able to afford to visit her much. However, I got why she wanted to go. That's where the next chapter of her story was. It was a strange thought, though, to think that once she left and Joanna went back to university, it would just be Katrina and I, and Jerry.

I had started back to school, and already the homework was building up. The summer heat proceeded despite the ending of my holidays, making the restriction of my shirt nearly unbearable.

As soon as I got home I changed, throwing on a pair of shorts and a loose T-shirt Joanna had bought me. Grabbing my book, I immediately headed back downstairs towards the front door.

I had read *Gulliver's Travels* twice since Mrs Vincent had given it to me, but going back to school had made me yearn for its adventure once more.

'Mrs Vincent! It's me!' I called, pushing open the heavy set front door.

'I'm in the kitchen. I'll be through in a minute, Jason,' she called back, the smell of fresh food wafting down the hall with her voice.

I made my way into the library. The room was dark, the curtains barely drawn. I placed my book on one of the armchairs and pulled the heavy curtains open.

'My gosh that's bright!' a voice exclaimed behind me.

I spun around, startled, jumping back against the window. It was Mr Vincent.

'Mr Vincent... I didn't realise you were in here. Sorry,' I stammered.

'Relax, boy,' he said, closing the book he was holding and placing it in his lap.

He stared off, seemingly mesmerised by a point far beyond

me. I remained standing, twiddling my hands awkwardly, hoping Mrs Vincent would appear any minute at the door.

'Well, don't stand on ceremony,' he laughed huskily, 'take a seat.'

I did as I was told, removing my book from the armchair, and replacing it in my lap once I was seated. We sat opposite each other, like the reflections of a mirror through time.

I couldn't remember the last time I had actually spoken to Mr Vincent. He tended to keep to himself. Katrina said the only people he really interacted with were his wife and the nurses who helped to take care of him.

'What are you reading?' I asked politely.

He inclined his head slightly, his eyes locked on me. I shifted uneasily in my seat. He grunted.

'What?'

A slight grin broke across his face, forcing the wrinkles around his eyes to deepen dramatically. 'She told me you had an interest in books. She also told me that she had got around to giving you that,' he pointed to the novel in my lap. My grip on the book tightened possessively.

'She told me you wanted me to have it now,' I replied quietly.

He chuckled his husky laugh. 'I did. The thing about this old person's disease is that you're never really sure when it's going to be the last time you can say your own name, let alone carry out something as important as giving you that battered old thing.'

I looked down at the book. I guess it was pretty battered; the front cover was torn at the corner, and some of the pages were crinkled, but in my eyes this made it even better; it meant he had read it, and read it more than once. It meant my dad had cherished it.

I raised my head, a lump forming in my throat, but curiosity building in my mind. 'Do you remember him, my dad?'

He watched me carefully. 'Not always,' he answered honestly, the candidness clear in his tone. He looked down, suddenly appearing more frail than the man who had startled me moments earlier. 'My memories fade in and out of clarity, you see. But I do remember his character.'

'What do you mean? What do you remember?'

'I remember that I liked him. I remember that he was kind, and I remember that he had a keen eye for the classics. But most importantly I remember that he always made an effort. He was always popping by, even though I knew that he had a house full of kids and a full-time job to tend to. But that never stopped him from visiting this old fool,' he laughed a crinkly-eyed smile, as he patted his chest in indication. 'I suppose it's the same for you, yes?'

'I... I'm not sure I know what you mean.'

'Well, you must have only been a small child when he passed,' he explained.

I felt a slight rush of heat inflame my cheeks.

'I suppose the memory of his character is all you have as well. I don't suppose you remember actually being with your parents, but that doesn't mean they are forgotten in memory. You remember their character, you remember their being, through what they did, and in the ways in which they live on. Through that book, for example, which was always his favourite. He told me he used to read it as a child.'

I sat in silence, watching him, my eyebrows furrowed together.

He chuckled to himself once more, before his expression grew suddenly solemn. He nodded subtly to himself, and then picking up his book and opening it to a marked page, he proceeded to read.

'*To Kill a Mockingbird*,' he said, a few moments later. 'That's what I'm reading.'

'I like that book,' I said. I paused for a few seconds, then opened my own book. 'Simon suggested it to me over the summer.'

'What do you think of Atticus's character?' he asked me, without raising his eyes from his page, but a smile breaking the solemnity that had appeared to momentarily take his expression hostage.

I smiled back, quickly returning my eyes to the page before answering.

Mrs Vincent came in shortly after. Something told me that she had been lingering intentionally outside the room, as she possessed a wry smile as she entered. She brought tea with her, and a glass of juice for me. She sat in the chair next to her husband. She pulled out a magazine from a slip-pouch on the side of the chair, and we all immersed ourselves in our individual reading.

Every so often I would notice Mr Vincent steal a look at Mrs Vincent. She would not return his look, but would reach out and gently squeeze his forearm, before letting her hand fall back to her lap.

If ever I had seen a look of unconditional love, it was that which he gave her. But there was something sad about his gaze. It reminded me of when you have a really great dream, but somewhere in your consciousness you know you will wake up, and so you know that you may not remember, that you may not feel what you are feeling in the moment. I turned my eyes back to my book.

The hours ticked by. Mr Vincent eventually decided to go upstairs to lie down for a bit, so I took that as my cue to leave.

'I hope he didn't talk your ear off,' Mrs Vincent laughed, as she walked me to the front door. 'I told him you were coming by and he was pretty eager to see you. I can't remember the last time he actually wanted to talk to someone that wasn't me.' She laughed again, patting her heart, just like I had seen her husband do.

'He asked me what I thought about *To Kill a Mockingbird*,' I told her, 'it turns out there's a lot more to the story than I thought. I think he understood it a lot more than I did.'

She paused, opening the door with her right hand as she rested her left on her hip. She smiled to herself; not the wry grin she so often wore, but a smile that indicated a more wistful feeling.

I paused by the open door, leaning into the breeze it offered. I placed one foot out of the door, ready to leave, but stopped myself as my sole touched the floor. Turning abruptly, I went to hug Mrs Vincent. I had never been very good at the whole talking thing, but I wanted her to know what I was thinking. I wanted her to know what Imogene hadn't: It's OK to not be OK.

I pulled back brusquely. 'He remembers you, you know. He may not always remember you *exactly*, but he remembers how much he loves you,' I said plainly, nodding my head emphatically. 'He'll always remember, deep down. I know he will.'

She smiled down at me, obviously taken aback, her lower lip quivering ever so slightly. I nodded at her and, saying goodbye, turned out the door. Something told me she wouldn't want me to see her cry.

I felt oddly proud of myself. My thoughts were flying as I tried to internalise what Mr Vincent had told me, what Mrs Vincent must be feeling, and what I myself was thinking. But I felt I had achieved something. I felt I had matured 100 years in a couple of hours.

'Hey little man,' a harsh voice said, breaking me out of my reverie as I strolled up our driveway.

I groaned internally. 'Imogene's at work,' I said hurriedly, not pausing as I proceeded to the door.

He stepped in front of me. I hadn't realised how tall he was; he towered over me. I frowned up at him, sighing heavily.

'Can I help you?' I said, tilting my head to the side, as I had seen Imogene do when she was obviously annoyed.

He smirked at me before leaning back against his car. Bits of red paint had faded away on the bonnet. The passenger's door on which he leant had an impressive dent in it.

'You're a funny kid aren't you?' he smirked, ruffling the hair at the back of his head. The bags under his eyes formed heavy, dark shadows. 'Listen, I was just looking for your sister, but if she's not here then I'll come back another time.'

He held his hands up, palms facing outwards, in a dramatic surrender, his smirk growing. He began to get in the car, pulling the creaky door open.

'What do you want to talk to her about?' I asked quickly.

He gave me a weary look, as if he was weighing me up. I disliked him more and more by the moment.

Theo ruffled his hair again. 'I just wanted to offer her my condolences.' He continued when I offered him nothing but a blank stare in response. 'With the whole job thing; the New York position. I know she tanked it. I thought I'd pop by to offer a few kind words.' He shrugged, his pleasant words not matching the harsh glint in his eyes.

My words flowed like angry lava. 'Yeah, well. She didn't tank the interview, actually. They gave her another chance,' I said, raising my chin proudly.

His smile grew but his overall expression hardened, making his whole being look nothing short of menacing. *What did she ever see in this guy?*, I thought to myself.

'Is that so?'

'Yep,' I continued, 'They obviously really liked her, because they gave her another audition, and she nailed it. I should know; she took me with her. So they'll probably give her the job.'

He nodded slowly, his forearm resting on the open car door. 'Huh.'

I remained where I stood, not quite sure what to do now.

'What are you reading?' he asked, indicating with a curt nod the book I still held in my hand.

Before I could answer he reached out, swiftly taking the book from my grasp. I called out, but he was already holding the book out of my reach. 'Oh, I remember this one. Good book,' he said, almost bored now. 'Well,' he sighed, 'I guess I'll have to offer Imogene my congratulations instead, then.'

I stood back, composing myself after trying and failing to reach my book. I held my hand out expectantly.

'Don't bother telling her I came by. I'll be back.' He threw the book in my direction, but the carelessness with which he did it caused it to spin through the air and land in a small puddle of dirty water that had formed at the foot of one of the rose bushes. 'Whoops.'

I heard the car door slam behind me, but I was already kneeling on the floor, grabbing the book from the murky water, and using the bottom of my T-shirt to wipe it clean.

My jaw was clenched tight as I fought back angry tears. I heard him drive away, exhaust fumes filling the air around me.

I *seriously* didn't understand what she had seen in him.

SIXTEEN

Joanna

The air blew briskly through my hair as I strode along the pavement. The schools had started back, so the streets were pretty empty. As I walked down the road to Abbey's house the only noise was the wind and the leaves, and my feet hitting the concrete. I arrived at her house within ten minutes of leaving mine.

She had called earlier this morning, saying she needed to talk to me. I left as soon as we hung up.

'Hey,' I greeted her as I walked through a side gate into her back garden. She was sitting on the patio on a faded white deck chair.

'Hey,' she replied, smiling up at me.

I sat in the chair next to her, as she positioned herself to look at me.

'Charlie quit her job at the restaurant,' she said ardently, throwing her hands out into the air dramatically. 'I don't know what happened. We had only just started our shift last night. You know, I haven't really spoken to her in a while, so I was trying to make conversation, asking her about what she had been up to, and she was so *blunt* with me. She was just being rude.'

'Why?' I asked, frowning suspiciously,

'I have no idea. I didn't bother pressing the matter. After

not talking to us after the party, it was kind of a slap in the face, so I just left her to it. The restaurant got busy so we didn't even have time to talk.'

'So what happened? Why did she quit?'

'She started arguing with one of the other waiters about something. I think it was about an order she had got wrong. Anyway, she started to get really angry, so my dad tried to sort it out, as she was causing a scene. But before anything could be resolved, she took off her apron and threw it in my dad's face. She quit, storming out and knocking a tray of glasses out of Rachel's hand before she left.'

I was stunned. 'What the hell?'

'I know, right.'

'Did you talk to her afterwards?' I asked, after a brief pause.

Abbey shook her head. 'I tried calling her but she never responded.'

Charlie hadn't spoken to me since the party, and I hadn't tried to reach out to her. I didn't know what Abbey expected of me. We sat in silence. I could practically hear the cogs turning in her brain.

'Maybe we should go by her house?' she suggested.

'OK,' I said, slapping my hands down on the chair as I pushed myself up.

As Abbey went to get her bag, my phone started ringing. It was Simon.

'Hey Simon.' I walked towards the door as I answered. 'What's up?'

'Hey. Are you free? Can we talk?' he sounded out of breath.

'Um… me and Abbey are just about to head over to Charlie's.'

'Charlie's actually the reason I'm calling. I ran into her in town today, and she was behaving really weirdly. She told me she quit her job.'

'Yeah, Abbey just told me. Did she seem OK to you?' I asked tentatively. His silence answered my question with more candour than words could have. 'We'll pick you up on the way to her house,' I told him.

'See you then,' he said grimly.

My stomach twisted into a ball of knots.

We got into Abbey's car, drove out of her cul-de-sace, and stopped by Simon's house.

'Hey guys,' Leo said, as he slid into the car alongside Simon. 'Mind if I come along?'

It didn't take us long to get to Charlie's house. She lived further out than the rest of us, but at the speed Abbey was nervously driving we got there in half the usual time. Charlie's house was a grand, detached house along a narrow street that led directly into the centre of town. She lived there with her mum and dad. It had countless rooms, extending down corridors, and up circling flights of stairs, but with only the three of them living there the grandness had a haunting quality. She rarely saw her mum and dad anyway; they were hardly ever at home, so she usually had the house to herself.

The driveway was empty except for a red Volvo parked at an angle in the middle. Abbey pulled in, just about managing to miss the front of the other car.

It had got colder, the hair on my arms standing up under the sleeves of my jacket. Leo swore loudly, as he stuck his hands into the pockets of his jeans, shivering. I fought back a smile as I proceeded up the steps to the front door. Simon stood directly behind me as I rang the doorbell. There was no answer, so after waiting a minute or so I rang again, but there was still no reply.

Simon sighed impatiently, and leaning past me opened the door himself. 'After you,' he said raising his eyebrows at me.

The knot in my stomach tightened as I walked ahead of

him. All of the lights inside appeared to be on, and the door was unlocked, and yet there was no sign of anyone.

'Charlie?' I called out.

'I think I hear someone upstairs,' Leo piped up, shutting the door behind him, blocking out the gusting wind.

'After you,' I said to Simon, indicating up the stairs with my hand. He smiled before placing his hand on the banister and heading upstairs.

Her house was only two storeys, so if there was someone inside they should have been able to hear us. I called out again, nonetheless. This time I heard what Leo must have heard; it sounded like the creaking of floorboards under the pressure of footsteps. Simon led us on to Charlie's room at the end of the corridor opposite the stairs.

'Who's there?' I heard Charlie shout, before breaking into a fit of giggles.

Simon looked back at me, a frown heavily imprinted upon his face.

I rushed forwards, moving past him, and swung her bedroom door open.

As I swung open the door I had to take a couple of steps into the room before I saw her sitting on the floor on the far side of the room. She was leaning back against the wall, but her head lolled forward as if she was struggling to keep control of her neck. She had a glass of dark liquid in her hand, and the room stank of alcohol.

Theo leaned against the wall next to her. He stood there with his arms crossed across his chest, seeming to measure each one of us up as we entered the room.

'What the hell is going on?' I moved quickly across the room to crouch down by Charlie. I took the glass from her hands, prying her tightly gripped fingers away. 'Is she drunk?' I asked Theo, turning my glare to him.

He remained blank-faced, staring down at me. The last

time I had seen him he tried to turn me against my sister, and now he appeared to be aiding the destruction of another person in my life.

'I think I can get myself drunk,' Charlie laughed loudly. I pushed back the tear-dampened strands of hair that covered her face. Her eyes couldn't settle, but instead roamed absently around the room.

'Getting drunk in the middle of the day. Nice,' Leo said, stepping forward. He didn't take his eyes off Theo. I had never seen Leo look so menacing; the gentleness of his face appeared to have been replaced by cold marble. He crossed his arms, accentuating their strong muscles.

Abbey bent down next to me. Charlie's wandering eyes found her, restarting the river of emotion that already stained her face.

'Oh Charlie,' Abbey whispered sadly, and Charlie began to weep.

'You should leave,' Simon said to Theo, the bluntness of his words matching the coldness of his eyes. '*Now.*'

Theo glanced briefly between Simon and Leo, who stood opposite him resolutely. Then his eyes moved slowly back down to me.

Charlie had rested her head on Abbey's shoulder and was softly crying into her jumper.

'Tell your sister I said hi,' he said, pushing himself forward from the wall.

I stood up, my chest rising up and down as angry breaths threatened to burst from me. 'Leave,' I said, throwing as much sternness into my voice as I could possibly manage.

He continued to stare at me, before moving his eyes down to my arm. I felt like the scars on my arm were burning anew under his gaze, before his eyes moved back up to meet mine.

'It's only a week until the anniversary, right? Don't worry,

I wouldn't miss it. I can't wait to see what Imogene does this time,' he sneered.

Before I could react, Simon moved past me. Grabbing the front of Theo's T-shirt with both hands, he threw him roughly up against the wall. I grimaced as I heard the back of Theo's head hit the wall. He didn't resist Simon, but instead let his arms fall limply to his sides. A grin spread across his face, as if he was enjoying how much he was getting to everyone.

Simon's knuckles whitened. 'Stay away from them. Do you hear me?'

'Bit protective, isn't he,' Theo laughed, raising his eyebrows at me.

Simon brought him forward before pushing him back against the wall again. 'Stay away from her.'

I stepped forward, placing my hand gently on Simon's shoulder. I could feel how tense he was beneath my touch. I didn't want it to escalate any further.

Simon let go of Theo's shirt, and moved back beside me. Theo walked past us and out of the room, his grin turning quickly to a sneer as he did so.

I exchanged a brief look with Simon, hoping it conveyed my thanks, before turning my attention back to the friend who sat broken on the floor.

Leo went and got Charlie a glass of water. When he came back, and after some coaxing, she sipped it slowly. We sat with her on the floor.

She had run into Theo after finishing a shift at the restaurant about a couple of weeks ago. She had recognised him from a party a couple of months earlier, as she knew one of his housemates. They had got talking and ended up going for a drink. She had been upset, and he had offered a listening ear. She told him about her break-up before summer, and in return he poured her a glass. They continued meeting up for the rest of the week.

She threw me a worried look, before burying her face in her hands and proceeding. Apparently, after she had found out about his involvement with Imogene, they had bonded over their mutual disdain.

He told her about the interview he had tried to sabotage. It was her idea for him to come to the house and tell me; she knew how I would react. She hoped I would push Imogene away.

'Why?' I asked incredulously, my voice coming out in almost a whisper. 'What have I ever done to you? Why?'

A lump rose in my throat, cutting me off. A mixture of betrayal and sadness hit me like a kick to the stomach. She was my friend; at least, she had been. Why would she actively seek to hurt my family?

'I don't know!' she exclaimed, throwing her hands up in the air, before running her fingers back through her tangled hair. She rested them there, intertwined in her black locks while she rested her head despairingly against the wall. 'I just…'

She clenched her jaw and swallowed before continuing. 'I haven't exactly been coping.' Fresh tears blurred her eyes, before spilling over onto the canvas of her cheeks. She looked around the room, her eyes still dazed. How much had she drunk?

'What do you mean? With what?' Abbey prompted, her voice kind and soothing.

Charlie let her hands fall into her lap, where she fidgeted with a thread from her jeans. She sighed again, but we didn't prompt her. We waited until she was ready to start talking again.

'I was afraid to tell you guys because you all seemed to be having so much fun. We all went off to uni, and yet I felt like the only one that hadn't been able to settle, hadn't been able to move on. As the year went on I thought things were getting better. I started doing well academically, I started seeing Jared, and I finally thought, *yes*, I have got my shit together.'

'Then you broke up,' Simon said quietly.

Charlie nodded. 'He ended things just like that' – she clicked her fingers – 'as if I was nothing. It was like I was just expendable. The friends I thought I had made turned their backs on me, sticking with him. I felt so alone,' she wept.

Then suddenly she stopped crying. She looked up and her face fell blank. 'But I thought as long as no one knew, it would be fine. Summer started, and I started hanging out with other people that I hadn't been friends with in school, people who didn't know me as well.'

'Why didn't you just talk to us about it?' Leo asked.

'I didn't want you guys to see how *pathetic* I was. That I let some guy push me over the edge.' She laughed sardonically. She looked back up at me, staring at me with pleading eyes. 'I saw Imogene at the start of the summer, the day after we had all been hanging out in your garden,' she cried, shaking her head. 'I can't say it. It's going to sound so horrible if I say it!'

'It's OK,' I lied. I squeezed her arm gently, and nodded at her. I knew I probably didn't want to hear what she had to say, but I knew she had to say it.

She broke her eyes away from me, favouring the sight of her lap. 'I knew how you had been struggling with her. I had watched it for years. So, when I saw her, I realised that at least there was someone more screwed up than I was.'

The rest of it came out in a flurry of fast-spoken words. 'I tried to reach out to Simon, but I knew… I knew I would never be his priority. That's why I lied to you at the party, Simon, because it finally clicked. I wanted someone else to hurt as much as I did, to feel more alone than I did. I thought maybe then I wouldn't feel so pathetic in comparison. I'm so, so sorry, Joanna. That's why I said what I did about her not really being part of your family, and that's why I got close to Theo.'

'I quit my job the day Abbey told me how you two were working things out. Not only had I isolated all of you guys, but I had turned into a *horrible* person in the process.'

I was stunned. She looked back up at me, her eyes searching mine. I didn't know what to say. So I didn't say anything. I pulled her into towards me. She wrapped her arms tightly around my neck, and she cried into my chest.

I kept my eyes open, frozen on the wall behind Charlie in a state of stunned confusion. I could see the others watching me in my peripheral vision. They couldn't possible figure out what was going through my mind, as I hadn't the slightest clue myself.

Charlie pulled away. Sighing, she shook her head. 'You guys must really hate me,' she said quietly.

'Well, its undeniable you've been a bitch recently, but I don't think we'd go so far as to say we *hate* you,' Leo joked.

Abbey threw him a warning look, nudging him with her elbow. But Charlie smiled, obviously appreciating the honesty.

'My parents don't know any of this by the way,' she said quickly. 'I lied to them about how well I've been doing at uni, and they haven't exactly been around enough this summer to catch me in a lie.' She laughed bitterly.

'Maybe you should try talking to them? Everyone has issues to deal with, and if they don't understand that then it's about time their glass house was shattered,' Simon added, a sly grin breaking his stony expression.

'Things aren't perfect between Imogene and I,' I said bluntly, looking Charlie in the eye. 'Despite what you might think. Yes, things haven't been this amicable between us in a very long time, but things are far from blissful. Things only started to get better when she decided to talk to me rather than use everyone as her emotional punch-bags. We all have shit to deal with, but that doesn't mean you have to deal with it alone.'

Abbey took my right hand in hers, breaking it away from

my scared arm, the very symbol of my demons. She smiled kindly at me.

'Is this the moment we all break into a joyous song about friendship and love?' Leo asked mockingly after a brief pause. 'It's just that, if so, I need to get my tambourine from the car.'

Abbey snorted loudly, which left the rest of us smiling, laughter breaking through the tension.

We stayed at Charlie's for the rest of the afternoon. She sobered up pretty quickly, aided by the food we eventually ordered. Intermittently someone would say something, getting something off their chest. Charlie talked to us a bit more about what had been going on with her, Leo told us how he was feeling the pressure of being at Cambridge, and Abbey related the pressure her parents were putting on her to go into the family business.

What was most surprising, though, was that Simon started telling us about how things with his mum were getting to him. Simon was reserved, he always had been, but opening up is like letting down the barrier of a dam: once it's down it's hard to stop the water from flowing. He only hinted at a few things, before quickly diverting the conversation away from himself, but it was enough. It was enough for me to see that there was still so much I didn't understand about him.

There was a lot I didn't understand about all of them.

SEVENTEEN

Imogene

Pulling my arm back, I sucked in a deep breath. I brought my arm down, then threw it forward, flicking my wrist. The pebble was launched from my hand into the entrapment of the waves. It skimmed the water twice before sinking out of sight.

I walked up the beach in search of another suitable pebble, picking them up and putting them back if they weren't flat enough. Giving up on finding the perfect pebble, I picked up the next one my hand touched, and with little thought I flung it at the ocean with all of the power I could transfer to my arm. It fell into the water with an audible splash, throwing droplets into the air.

The wind picked up, throwing ringlets of my hair into my face. I drew my hair back and tied it up, before strolling further down the beach.

Closer to the water's edge, I found a rock large enough to lean up against. Digging my hands into the warmth of my jacket pockets, I sat with my legs crossed under me, leaning back against the rock. The cold air hit my face, but I didn't mind. It felt kind of nice, as it made me appreciate the warmth from within my jacket even more.

I hadn't spoken to anyone today; Katrina was at work, Jason was at school, and Joanna was out with friends. I did have

Jerry, though. I had never particularly bonded with the dog, but when Jason wasn't around he seemed to favour following me instead. He had followed me down to the beach, and was splashing about at the water's edge. Whenever he wandered too far out of sight, I would whistle for him, and he would come running back as fast as his old legs would carry him.

Tomorrow was the anniversary.

Things had been better over the past few weeks; much better than they had been in years. I smiled wryly at the truth of this thought. I honestly couldn't remember the last time I had been on good terms, at this time of year, with the people for whom this event also held significance.

Things seemed so much simpler.

Yet, as time went on, I felt that I was becoming more fragile. I would never admit it, but it felt that as time went on, and things continued to get better, a piece of me was just sitting back, waiting for the perfect moment to self-destruct; a moment that had yet to present itself.

I sighed as I pushed this thought from my mind. I whistled, and Jerry came running to me. Dripping wet, he lay down next to me. I took one hand from my jacket pocket and placed it on his damp fur. Closing my eyes, I rested my head back.

I made myself blind to every sight around me, deaf to every noise, and oblivious to every thought that tried to break into my mind. I simply wanted to sit.

Jerry started barking.

Looking up, I groaned internally. Someone was walking across the beach towards me.

'Good morning, Imogene,' Mrs Vincent called when she got closer.

I waved languidly. Jerry remained where he was, apparently bored of the human world.

'Bitter day, isn't it,' she said once she got over to where I remained sitting. She bounced up and down on the balls of her feet, trying to keep herself warm. 'It definitely is the end of summer. It's meant to rain as well tomorrow.'

'So I heard,' I replied, squinting up at her, before looking down at the pebbled sand.

'I haven't seen you in a while. How are things?' she asked, politely.

'Just peachy, thanks,' I replied, maybe a bit too sarcastically.

But just as I thought, she didn't appear put off. Instead, a playful grin played around the corners of her mouth, deepening the wrinkles around her lips. 'Mind if I join you?' she asked, obviously rhetorically, as she sat down before I had a chance to answer.

'It's so peaceful down here isn't it,' she said amiably, looking over at me.

I nodded in agreement. Jerry got up and lay down again on a patch of soft sand further up the beach. Some seagulls rested tranquilly on the water in front of us, but the waves were getting rougher.

A moment of silence passed between us.

Mrs Vincent chuckled softly.

'What's the joke?' I asked, turning my head towards her.

'I was just thinking about the first time you came to the beach. Do you remember?' she asked, smiling in reminiscence.

'The first day we moved here.' Freeing my hand from my pocket I picked up a small pebble and launched it into the water. 'Vera and Benson brought us down here, while we waited for the delivery truck.'

She smiled and nodded. I sighed and reluctantly smiled too. 'We met you and Mr Vincent for the first time.'

'And if I remember correctly, you ran straight into the water. Your mum told you not too, but you didn't listen,' she laughed. 'We all thought you were in trouble, until your dad ran into the waves after you, splashing around like he was a child himself.'

I shook my head laughing, getting lost in her memory. 'I'd forgot about that. Vera had to stop Joanna from running in after us.'

The wind picked up, blowing loose strands of my hair into my face. Mrs Vincent appeared unperturbed, her French plait hanging perfectly over her shoulder.

My smile faded and I breathed in the brisk air. It definitely felt like the change of seasons.

'How is Mr Vincent?' I asked, after another pause. I started drawing pictures with my fingers in a patch of sand beside me.

'He's OK,' she replied, her tone implying she didn't mean 'OK' in the traditional sense of the word. 'And how are things at home?'

'OK,' I said, mimicking her use of the word.

She smiled wryly, shaking her head slightly from side to side. I smiled before looking back down at my fingertips dancing in the sand.

'OK, then,' she said nodding her head conclusively.

At that moment I couldn't actually remember the last time I'd had a cordial conversation with the woman who sat to my left.

'Thank you,' I said, almost reluctantly.

'For what?' she asked, frowning confusedly.

I threw another stone at the water, but it fell short and landed among other pebbles. I indicated ambiguously with my hand towards our house. 'For being there for Joanna and Jason.'

'It's been lovely sharing our library with Jason this summer...'

'That's not what I mean,' I interrupted her bluntly. 'Not just this summer, but the past nine years,' I said miserably. *For doing what I apparently hadn't been able to*, I thought.

'You really are too harsh on yourself, aren't you?' was all she said in response.

I frowned at her. 'Excuse me?'

'Don't get me wrong, you haven't exactly been an angel over all the years I've known you,' she continued.

'I presume you have a point?'

She chuckled quietly, but I sat there frowning at her.

'You should be proud of yourself, is what I'm trying to say. I'm definitely proud of you,' she said, smiling gently over at me.

'What exactly do you think I should be proud of?'

She pushed herself off of the ground, breathing heavily with the effort. Once she was standing, she dusted sand off her legs, before resting her hands on her hips. She looked as if she had just landed in the New World. She looked slightly crazy. She looked resilient, her feet planted in the sand as if she was exactly where she wanted to be.

'You've done more than most have; you've been through the rabbit hole and made it out the other end,' she said, no longer smiling, but now seemingly sombre in her being.

She turned to walk away, but suddenly turned back in an exclamation of remembrance.

'Oh, I almost forgot,' she said, reaching into her coat pocket. 'A woman came by earlier. She had bright red hair. She knocked on your door, but no one was in. She wanted to deliver a letter. It seemed important, so I said I would deliver it for her. It's addressed to you.'

She handed me an envelope with my full name printed formally on the front.

'Thanks,' I said, already prying open the envelope.

She nodded and walked away, back down the beach. Jerry raised his head to look at her, before laying it back down.

I gave up trying to open the envelope neatly, and ripped it open.

I had been expecting a call from Miss Carson, or Mr Jepsen, but I had received none. It was nearly a month since I had met with them. She had emailed me that day, saying that they had a full schedule of other meetings over the next few weeks, but that they would definitely get in contact with me. Apparently they had finally proven true to their word.

Once I had freed the contents, I screwed up the empty envelope and put it in my coat pocket. Adrenaline flew through my veins as my eyes skimmed the page. I was oblivious to the world around me; to everything but the ink on the page.

I must have read the letter about five times before I finally let my hand fall to my side, the letter still in my grasp. My eyes remained frozen on my lap, locked on the place where I had read the letter.

I didn't feel anything.

The glue I had used to put myself back together was no longer strong enough. Who had I been kidding?

She was probably relieved that no one was at the house; it's easier to deliver bad news when you aren't actually required to deliver it.

It felt as if I was going to cry. I didn't.

I thought I was going to scream, to cry out. I didn't.

I hadn't realised how much I actually wanted it.

I laughed bitterly. 'Well now you know,' I said quietly to myself. I stuffed the letter into the pocket with the envelope.

Out of one rabbit hole, and into the next.

EIGHTEEN

Joanna, the Anniversary

I stayed in bed. I was awake, but that didn't mean I wanted to get up. I had my eyes open, staring at my ceiling. I really needed to repaint it.

Jason had left for school, and Katrina for work. *Imogene must still be in bed too*, I thought. I hadn't seen her since yesterday morning.

'Knock, knock.' Abbey emerged through my bedroom door.

I sat up quickly pushing the blankets down away from my head. 'Hey,' I said, frowning with surprise.

She half-jogged, half-skipped across the room. 'Budge up,' she said, pulling back the covers before climbing under them.

I moved across slightly and turned on my side so that I was facing her. She lay on her back, and turned her head to me with a smile. 'You know, you really should lock your front door when everyone else is out.'

'Lesson learned,' I said, pulling the covers back up under my chin.

I heard a bang downstairs, like a cupboard door slamming shut.

'Leo and Simon,' Abbey nodded, answering my unvoiced question.

'Does that mean I have to get out of bed?' I asked, burying myself deeper into the cave of my duvet cover.

'Food's ready!' someone yelled from downstairs.

'Only if you want to eat,' she replied, pushing herself into a sitting position. She smiled again, before surveying me more seriously. Pushing her glasses up, she asked, 'Did you get any sleep at all?'

I shook my head.

She nodded understandingly, before jumping out of the bed. 'Come on,' she said, before disappearing out of the room. I sighed and followed.

For the first couple of years after the accident we all tended to keep to ourselves on the anniversary date. I don't think Jason fully grasped the reason until he was older, but he came to recognise this date as one weighed down with a melancholic significance.

It wasn't until I was about sixteen that Katrina started to occupy us. One year she took us to the beach and showed us how to make a bonfire; the tradition stuck. We sat, we talked, we laughed, we had food; it was nice. However, Imogene didn't care for this tradition. Sometimes she would make an appearance, but never in a way which caused us to wish she would stick around. But I knew this year would be completely unique. Everyone was in such a different place.

Katrina called me later in the afternoon to say she was on her way home, and that she was going to pick Jason up on her way. Abbey, the others and I made our way down to the beach.

Near where the path from our house met the sand of the beach, was a fire-pit. It had been there as long as I could remember. Surrounding the pit were three driftwood benches, making a horseshoe shape encircling the fire, with the opening of the horseshoe facing the sea.

Simon and I began building the fire. Leo lounged back on one of the benches, his arm around Abbey. After a while we managed to get the fire going, and Simon smiled broadly, proud of his creation. However, we needed more wood if we wanted to keep it alight, so Abbey volunteered to go back to the house, and Leo unsurprisingly volunteered to keep her company. I didn't know when they had become official in their relationship, but they definitely seemed to have no qualms about being open with it now.

Simon and I sat back on one of the driftwood benches, relishing the heat of the small fire.

'When do you leave for uni?' Simon asked me, burying his hands into his coat pockets.

'In about a month. What about you?'

'The same, I think,' he nodded. 'So, when are you going to tell the others about your tattoo?'

I spun around to stare at him, my eyes widening. 'What?'

His face broke into a sheepish grin. 'I noticed the design on your desk a couple of weeks ago, and you've been wearing long-sleeved tops a lot lately.'

'It's cold recently,' I said, blankly.

'Well, I didn't know for sure, but your reaction just confirmed it,' he laughed again. His grin softened. 'I won't tell the others.'

'Thank you.'

'But I am curious,' he continued.

I laughed, 'Curiosity killed the cat.'

'Unless the cat fights back,' he retorted, raising his eyebrows.

Just then Leo came running back to where we sat around the bonfire. He was panting, his feet throwing up sand as they hit the ground with speed. I stood up as soon as I noticed him running towards us.

'Leo...?'

He didn't let me finish. 'Joanna, you need to come back to the house. Imogene's home, and she's going crazy. Katrina and Jason are back, and they're trying to calm her down.'

I stumbled forwards a few steps before breaking into a

sprint. I didn't ask any questions, and Leo and Simon followed silently behind me. We left the warm, amber glow of the fire behind us. Leo's words had sparked nothing short of pure panic within me.

I threw open the wooden gate at the back of our garden, and it slammed back against the fence. As we sprinted up through the garden to the back patio doors of the house, I could hear glass breaking. I could hear yelling.

'What the hell…?' I stammered as we stumbled into the wreckage of the kitchen.

Shattered glass littered the floor, and Imogene stood amongst the wreckage. Katrina stood near the door, still wearing her coat, with her handbag slung over her shoulder. Jason stood to the right of the door in front of Abbey. She had her arms wrapped around his chest. He was staring, startled, at Imogene.

'Imogene, what's going on?' I asked her, my voice seeming to break into the chaos like a feather in a storm.

She laughed. She actually shook her head at me and *laughed.* Her face was clearly tear-stained, strands of her hair glued to her face by her apparent despair. She was breathing heavily, but her face was contorted as if she were struggling to control the air escaping her.

I looked at Katrina, searching her being for an explanation, but she did nothing more than mirror my confusion.

Katrina broke the silence that fell once Imogene had stopped laughing. 'Imogene, you need to calm down. If something's happened… whatever is going on…'

'Then what, Katrina?' Imogene breathed out exasperated. 'How are you going to fix it?' She raised her eyebrows at our aunt. She sighed heavily, and leaning forward she placed her hands on the kitchen island in front of her. A piece of paper was gripped in her right hand.

'Imogene, what happened?' I asked, louder this time, stepping over the debris from a broken plate.

She bolted upright, waving the piece of paper in her hand. 'I tried,' she began. Her face softened and her frustration flowed freely down her cheeks. 'I really tried to sort myself out.' She sighed laboriously. 'I didn't get the job. They believed that despite my *obvious talent*, that I was not a *suitable contender.*'

'Oh, Imogene,' Katrina said, stepping forward. 'They'll be other chances.'

'It's not just about the job though, is it,' I said, looking hard at Imogene. I shook my head, as my eyes began to fill with tears. 'You wouldn't have chosen today to do this if it was just about a fucking job.'

'Joanna!' Katrina warned me.

My eyes were locked on Imogene's. She nodded slightly at me.

'You pulled me out of the car,' she whispered, tears dripping down off of her chin. 'I could never remember what had happened. We never spoke about it, and I never remembered. You pulled me out of the car, didn't you?'

'What?' My voice was incredulous, my face crumpled with disgust and frustration.

My chin began to quiver, and my chest rose and fell as the sobs threatened to break me. My fingernails dug into my scars.

She continued quietly. 'I was just as pathetic as I am now. You pulled Jason from the car…'

'You couldn't hold it together for one more day!'

'… and then you pulled me out too.'

'Imogene, enough!' I was almost screaming. It was as if I was no longer in control of myself.

'You couldn't help them, but you got us out!' She shook her head and took a step back from me. 'I couldn't save you, but you saved us. That's how you got your scar,' she wept. 'I couldn't save you… and you couldn't save them.'

'Shut up!' I screamed hysterically.

Simon came up behind me, and held my shoulders, rooting me where I was.

'You tried but you couldn't save them. That's why you forgot. You didn't want to remember. You chose us,' she whispered. 'You wanted me to be your knight in shining armour, because you thought it went hand in hand with the villain, that being responsible for saving two lives also meant you were responsible for the loss of two. But it wasn't your fault,' she wept. 'It was mine.'

'Imogene, enough!' Katrina said firmly, tears brimming in her eyes as she stepped closer to us.

Imogene just continued to stare at me. It was as if she was broken; the only thing rooting her to the ground was the meeting of our eyes.

She shrugged her shoulders, her expression a passive mask, the hysterics which only seconds ago had gripped her suddenly wiped away. 'At least you tried,' she shook her head. 'It was more than I ever did.'

'Just stop it!' I yelled again.

My body weakened as I drowned in my tears. Simon put his hand on my waist and hugged me into him. I think he was the only reason I stayed standing. I leaned into him.

'What do you mean?' Jason asked quietly, pulling himself from Abbey's hands to stand closer to Imogene.

'I'm so sorry, Jason,' Imogene began to weep again, intensely, as her eyes fell on our little brother. 'It's all my fault. It was all my fault!'

Imogene's hands flew up and she gripped her hair with her hands. Katrina went to pull her hands down, calling for her to calm down. Imogene pushed Katrina back with significant force, and she fell back against the counter, gripping the side to catch herself. Leo stepped up to Imogene, bracing himself.

'I'm the reason the car crashed. I was yelling at him. I was always arguing with them. He wasn't paying attention to the road because of me,' she said quietly, shaking her head frantically as she looked back and forth between Jason and I.

'Imogene, it wasn't your fault,' Simon said firmly. 'It was an accident. There was another car,' he said bluntly, offering her this explanation.

'Why were you yelling at them?' Jason suddenly shouted.

We turned to him and his face was flushed with anger. 'Why do you always have to ruin everything?' he yelled again, his hands balled into fists.

'Jason, I'm sorry!' Imogene stammered.

It was too late.

'I hate this!' he shouted, before turning and running from the kitchen. 'I hate all of it!'

I pulled myself free from Simon and ran after him, shouting his name. I heard people yelling after us. He got to the front door before me, and the wind blew the rain at me as I barrelled through the open door.

I hadn't even noticed it had started raining, but now my lashes fought against the obscurity of the falling droplets.

I ran across the driveway, my feet pounding hard against the ground. But I didn't feel it. I didn't feel the rain as it hit my face, nor the wind as it threw my hair back. I didn't hear the voices calling behind me. All I knew was Jason's figure as he ran across the road away from the house.

He was the last thing I saw.

Bright lights flew at me, breaking suddenly through the curtains of rain. Tyres squealing on the wet ground… but they weren't slowing down. A beaten-up red Volvo, and then hands grabbing me, pushing.

'Joanna!'

Screaming, crying, a blazing pain biting my left arm, and a sister's sacrifice.

The blackness took me.

NINETEEN

Imogene

'Imagine if a hooded man came up to you, handed you a giant leather-bound book and smiled, walking away without a single word. You begin to read it and you realise that this is a book of your entire life. From beginning to end, birth to death, every single event, every fear, every smile, moment of laughter, and of love written down. What would you do? Would you read it to the end?' Joanna had asked me this one day.

I'm sure if she had known how the summer would unfold she wouldn't have hesitated to skim through the pages to its end.

Or would she? Would she have wanted to know?

Would I?

When she had posed the question to me I had laughed, and told her I didn't have time. I had brushed her off. What she probably hadn't realised is just how deeply a question like that could make unwanted thoughts resurface. How it could make me face the demons I had tried so hard to keep buried.

By the end of the summer I had set fire to so many pages of my story that I just couldn't salvage the chapters I had yet to read.

Nine years ago my parents died. Nine years ago my world fell apart. What the future held seemed irrelevant.

We had been coming home from the Taylors' house. I had been arguing with Benson and Vera all day. Joanna told me to stop, but she couldn't understand. They just wouldn't tell me. No matter how many times I asked them, they just wouldn't tell me what had happened to me before they adopted me. They wouldn't tell me anything. It began with simple curiosity, but it developed into so much more. I persisted because I began to notice the differences. I didn't look anything like them.

On the day of the accident I had been particularly persistent. I knew it would upset them but I didn't care. Why did I never care?

The roads were dark, deserted. He drove with both of his hands on the steering wheel. I lost my temper. I yelled at him, and he spun around in his seat. He took his eyes off the road and a hand off the steering wheel.

He didn't see it coming because my anger demanded his full attention.

The other car skidded out of control.

Perhaps it still would have hit us. Perhaps they still would have died.

Sadly, my story doesn't deal out answers to hypotheticals. It simply proves that there are no bystanders; everybody plays a part. I cast myself as the villain. I played my part.

Joanna reacted quickly. Jason screamed. He screamed so loudly. She got him from the car, while I drifted in and out of the blackness. Then she came back for me.

I screamed at her to check Mum and Dad. I screamed at her to check that they were OK. I threw my arm out to push her away from me. She cut her arm along the glass. I shoved her towards the infliction of her scars. The jagged edges of the broken window bit at her arm, and licked at the blood that flowed down her pale skin.

She undid my seatbelt, put my arm over her shoulder, and helped me from the car.

I don't know when the fire started, but it was hungry.

Someone called for help. Someone wrapped me in a foil sheet. But it was the policeman with the fluffy white hair who brought us to Katrina.

I never saw the driver of the other car. He was simply another victim of my story.

I blocked out as much as I could. I tried to hide the demons of my memory in the caves of my mind. But the more you try to lock things away, the harder they try to escape.

I never meant to be so hard on Joanna, on Jason and on Katrina, and even on Simon. I just didn't know how to tell them. I didn't know how to tell them that I was sorry, because I had never managed to conquer goodbye.

The details of my pain were forgotten in memory, but the characters of my future faced the consequences.

The rain beat hard against my face. I blinked ferociously through it. I screamed for Joanna and Jason. I ran after them.

I heard the others call out behind me. I felt Simon as he tried to pull me back by my arm. My demons laughed at the irony; I had caused my brother and sister to run from the house, and yet I hoped to catch them.

I saw the headlights. I saw Joanna freeze in the road. I saw that the car didn't slow down. Why didn't it slow down?

I ran forward. I lost all consciousness of what I was doing, but I felt my actions, and I believed in them with every ounce of my being.

'Joanna!' someone screamed behind me.

My body screamed so my voice didn't have to. I ran forward. I held my hands out. They collided with Joanna, and I pushed. I forced her body away from me. I pushed my sister away from me, and the car applauded me with the cold metal of its bonnet.

I didn't want to play the villain any more.

TWENTY

Simon

I know how clichéd it sounds, but I really do hate hospitals. It wasn't even the sterility of the surfaces, or the ugliness of the patterned curtains separating the beds, that made me cringe the minute I entered the institution's door. I didn't even mind the stinging smell of disinfectant. It was the people. Every person I passed, everyone I made passing eye contact with, made heat rush up my neck and put my nerves on edge. They could be smiling, crying, laughing, or wailing, but it all made me want to turn around and walk back out of the doors.

The person I just held the door open for, or the woman I just passed in the corridor, or the nurse I just asked for directions, could be dealing with the biggest battle of their lives, and I had no idea. There was nothing I could do.

Now I was waiting in a waiting room on the third floor – or was it the second? – to find out if my best friend and her sister were still alive.

I *hate* hospitals.

Leo paced the floor in front of me, and Abbey sat with her face buried in her hands, glancing up at the door erratically. I sat furthest away, completely still. I didn't pace the floor, I didn't want to burry my face in my hands, or bounce my leg in nervous agitation. I didn't talk, and I wasn't listening. I simply waited to be awoken from the nightmare I had been thrust into.

There was still no sign of Jason.

Katrina had gone in the ambulance with Imogene, and I went with Joanna. Leo and Abbey had stayed behind to look for Jason, but had been unlucky. They had called on Mrs Vincent and she was keeping an eye out to see if he turned up. Once in the waiting room, I had called my mum. She had joined the search too.

If only I had been faster. If only I had been quicker to stop him running out of the door. I still felt the fabric of Imogene's sleeve escape through my fingertips as I tried to pull her back.

I really fucking hate hospitals.

As the door to the waiting room swung open Katrina emerged, backed by an orchestra of raindrops hitting the windows around us.

Abbey's head jerked upwards, and Leo spun around, stopping dead in his tracks. I remained where I sat.

Leo was the first to speak. 'Are they…'

She cut him off. 'Joanna's OK. She's still in and out of consciousness, but they said she should be OK,' she smiled, but her tired eyes drew her young face down.

'But Imogene's injuries are far worse.' She swallowed. 'They said the internal bleeding was pretty bad,' she said, indicating her own abdomen, as if she was trying to understand it herself by explaining it to us. 'They said we'll have to wait a bit longer to know if she's OK.' She stuttered on the last word.

Abbey rose and pulled Katrina into a hug. 'Joanna's OK,' she smiled over Katrina's shoulder. Then nodding her head fervently, she added with naive optimism, 'So Imogene will be too.'

Katrina didn't look convinced, but patted Abbey appreciatively on the arm. She then turned to me. I found her eyes, but my words remained lost.

She nodded slightly. Brushing her hair back, and pushing

it tightly behind her ears, she said, 'I think we should let Jo sleep for now. I don't want to overwhelm her. Is there any word about Jason?' She looked fretfully between us all, her lower lip quivering as she breathed heavily in and out, as she tried to remain in control of herself.

I shook my head. 'My mum hasn't found him, and Mrs Vincent said she hasn't seen him, but she's still keeping an eye on your street.'

'We checked his friend Ben's house, and Ben's mum said she would call around some other families from his school,' Abbey added.

'The police said they would let us know if they find him,' was Leo's contribution.

Katrina nodded, as if this was all very useful information, but her face remained the same contorted mask of despair. Her lip trembled even more, and tears escaped down her face. 'Shit,' she whispered, spinning in a circle where she stood. 'This is all my fault.'

'Stay with Joanna. Tell us if anything progresses with Imogene. We'll go back out and look. I can think of a few other places he might go,' I said, standing up. I walked stiffly across the room.

Katrina nodded quickly at me. 'OK. OK, yes, let's do that.' She looked at me once more, then hugged me quickly, before walking out of the door and in the direction of Joanna's room.

I let out a deep sigh, but it only made a miniscule dent in the tiredness gripping me.

We made our way down into the foyer of the hospital. A woman in a wheelchair was being pushed by an elderly man. A guy, who can't have been much older than us, was walking in holding the hand of a little girl. She was wearing pyjamas under her coat, and didn't stop coughing as they walked past. She sleepily rubbed her eyes with her balled-up fists. The rain lashed at the glass entrance.

We paused in the foyer as we did up our coats.

'Guys!' Charlie came speedily walking over to us across the foyer. She stopped in front of us. Her hair was slicked against her head and her coat was drenched from the rain. 'I was just coming up to see you guys. My phone died, that's why I didn't get your messages,' she said, flustered, indicating to Abbey. 'What the hell happened? Are they OK? Have you heard anything? Where are you going?' she frowned as the questions spilled from her lips.

I told her that Joanna was going to be OK, but that she was unconscious again when we left Katrina. I told her that Imogene was still in a critical condition, and then I told her that we were going to go find Jason, that no one had heard from him since he had run out of the house.

He wasn't there when the ambulances came. Did he even know that his sisters had been hit? What was going through his head? How much of the accident did he see? Did he see it? I found it hard to believe that if he had, he would have continued to run.

'Shit…' was all she whispered in response, drawing the word out.

It seemed to be the best word to describe the situation.

'I'll come and help you guys look, then,' she added, zipping her coat back up.

'We have two cars between us. Leo and I can go back into town, and check in with a few more of his friends,' Abbey said definitively. 'Why don't you two go back to the house and see if he's got back home yet?'

I nodded solemnly. Charlie nodded enthusiastically, looking back and forth between us all. I moved to walk towards the door, but Abbey grabbed my arm. She pulled me into a tight hug, wrapping her arms firmly around my neck.

'She's OK, Simon. Jo's still here.' She whispered this in my ear.

I felt part of my inner being relax at this affirmation, and I put my arms around her to hug her back. She gave me one last squeeze before letting go.

We said goodbye, and split up to find our cars in the car park.

The wind beat against the car windows like pieces of broken glass. The image of Imogene smashing into the windshield of that car flew into my mind. The glass had showered the road like crystal teardrops. She had lain listless amongst them, as if they had exploded from her very being.

My grip tightened on the steering wheel. The rain hit the windows harder.

We had been sitting in silence as Charlie and I made our way from the hospital grounds. Sitting in the passenger seat, she had both of her knees tucked up towards her chest. One hand rested on the chair, palm down, the other held her neck as she looked out of the window.

'I couldn't believe my ears when Abbey called me,' she began, shaking her head vigorously. 'It's insane,' she continued, looking to me to feed the conversation. I didn't.

I turned left down a side road that would allow us to bypass the town centre.

'Did you see the driver? Did anyone? To hit her like then and then drive off... What a sick son of a bitch,' she said bitingly, shaking her head vigorously. 'At least Joanna's OK,' she said, quieter. 'And I'm sure Imogene...' She didn't finish.

'You really love her, don't you?' she whispered, her head resting back against the window. 'Them. They're lucky to have you,' she said, so quietly I almost didn't hear her.

I glanced briefly over at her. She looked thinner, her face worn down by fragility. My grip on the steering wheel loosened momentarily, but I swallowed my feelings back, and my grip strengthened as we barrelled down the dark night roads.

Then with my left hand I reached over and took her hand

in mine. I squeezed it briefly. She looked over at me and smiled genially. After a brief pause she nodded subtly, and squeezed my hand in return. I took my hand back and returned it to the steering wheel.

'He's probably hiding in his room, wondering what on earth is going on,' she said, as we pulled down their street.

I really hope she's right.

I parked about half a mile up the street from their house. Shattered glass still dusted the scene of the accident, and a wall of police tape formed a cage around it.

None of us had given the police much to go on. None of us recognised the car. None of us saw the licence plate, or the driver. It had been like a red bullet of agony; it had hit its target and continued flying.

Leo and Abbey had mostly been the ones to deal with them. The police had met Katrina at the hospital briefly, but there was only so much she could tell them.

I only allowed myself a quick glance at the road as we walked past. The rain lashed against my eyes. I hadn't bothered to put my hood up. Charlie ran towards the door ahead of me. I found the spare key from within the mouth of an ugly ceramic frog that sat on the front step.

I unlocked the door and walked into the hall. Charlie slammed the door shut behind us, exerting effort against the wind which wished to keep it open.

I took a deep breath as I surveyed the house in front of me, exhaling shakily.

She's OK. Jo's still here.

But is Imogene?

TWENTY ONE

Jason

Jerry raised his head from my lap, surveyed the sparse attic, and then rested his head on the cold wooden floor. I racked my brain to remember the last time I had been in our attic.

My hair was still wet, but my clothes were almost dry. I had grabbed a blanket from the bathroom before I had come up here.

For a while I had just wandered around. I didn't stop running until I physically couldn't any more. I had sat in a bus stop for a while, but the wind was a persistent ally of the rain and it found me even when I was curled up within the shelter. I only came back here when the rain got too heavy and I realised I wasn't wearing a waterproof coat.

When I got back to the house no one was here. I used the back door, using the beach path to get to the garden. I fished my key out of my pocket and let myself in. The lights were off and no one was in. I didn't complain. I didn't know where they were, but them simply being elsewhere was enough for me.

I didn't like to swear. When Imogene got angry she swore. Katrina swore accidently upon occasion, but always reprimanded herself when she was with me. I personally didn't really care if people swore, but I just never really felt the need. Why did that one word allow you to process your anger any more than another?

After getting a blanket from the bathroom, I called for Jerry. He came without hesitation. I didn't feel like being found so I made my way up here.

There was a small, steep flight of stairs leading up here, just next to Joanna's room. We never used it and we never came up here. I once even forgot it existed. It was mostly just filled with boxes, and bags of old clothes, stuff Katrina said we would probably find a use for one day.

I sat between a box of skiing clothes and a pile of dusty blankets. I wrapped my blanket tightly around me, pulling my knees up to my shoulders, and Jerry lay with his head resting upon me.

'Shit,' I said aloud. It didn't work; I was still just as angry.

I wasn't even sure angry was the right way to describe how I was feeling. Frustrated, disappointed, resentful, and yet expectant seemed more appropriate. After all, had I really expected anything less from tonight?

They were probably still out looking for me, and I wondered how long it would take for that bunch of geniuses to figure out I had come home.

The front door slammed. Jerry's head rose again, a low growl fluttered from his mouth. I put my hand on his head to quieten him.

If they are all downstairs, Imogene probably isn't among them, I thought. After the way she had behaved, she had probably run off to stay with one of her deadbeat mates, like she always did. Joanna would be crying, Katrina would be trying to hold everyone together.

I, however, didn't appear to have played my usual part in this charade; when Imogene and Joanna were fighting, something had snapped in my head. I'd had enough. I didn't want to repeatedly witness them tearing each other – and themselves – apart. They all got to go about their normal, adult, lives when tonight was over. I was a kid, and yet the adults were the ones making a mess of things.

I stayed quiet, and stretched out my legs on the floor. I wasn't going to help them find me. Jerry laid back on my lap, but continued to growl protectively.

'Jason! Are you here?' Simon yelled repeatedly.

Jerry's growl ceased. I sighed heavily.

'Ja-a-so-o-n!' a girl's voice – it sounded like Charlie's – shouted, elongating each syllable.

I heard them walking about the house, and eventually heard the creaking floorboards of the attic staircase.

The door swung open and Charlie and Simon emerged into the cold room.

Simon stood holding the door knob, his breathing heavy. He surveyed me silently, his eyebrows cemented in a deep frown. 'Thank God,' he said quietly.

Charlie walked further into the room, moving around Simon's motionless figure. 'We've being looking for you. Are you OK?' she asked tentatively.

I stared back at them silently, before dropping my eyes to Jerry's head, which I stroked back and forth.

'What happened to you? Where did you go?' she pressed, walking towards me before kneeling down about a metre in front on me.

At my lack of response she sighed impatiently, and looked up at Simon.

Simon closed the door behind him, before walking slowly over to me. Picking up the pile of blankets to my left, he moved them to one side before sitting in their place. He rested his head against the wall and bent one knee up, resting his arm on it.

He turned his head to look at me. 'I'm not surprised you ran off. I probably would have. But you should have let us know you were OK.'

I rolled my eyes internally. Externally my face remained stony.

'Jason,' Simon began, but his voice cracked.

I looked up at him and he averted his eyes.

'Are the others OK now?' I asked quietly, even though I knew this could never be true in the full sense of the word.

'There was an accident after you ran off.'

He rubbed his face with his palm roughly, before telling me everything.

My blood ran through my veins like ice-cold water. My senses deafened to all but the raindrops erratically hitting the roof tiles above my head.

'We didn't know if you saw what happened – if you knew…' He looked at me searchingly, his jaw clenched tight.

I shook my head, my jaw trembling.

The rain had been so loud… the wind… Once I ran over the road, I ran through the alley by the Coopers' house, as it was a short cut to the next block. I heard shouting. I heard them call for me. Then they stopped. I thought they had just given up. I told Simon and Charlie this. The rain had been so loud.

'I don't understand,' I stammered, tears freely rolling down my cheeks. 'I don't understand…'

Simon put a hand on my shoulder and tried to help me see through the storm that was blurring my mind. 'When we left the hospital we were told that Joanna is going to be OK. She's in and out of consciousness, but she will be… OK. Imogene… she was hit badly. She was still in surgery when we left.'

'Why don't we go to the hospital?' Charlie said, patting my knee as she smiled encouragingly, soberly.

I looked at her smile, but I didn't believe it. Smiling is like swearing in that way; it's not real. Swearing doesn't make you angry, and smiling doesn't make you happy. Tears, however, are far more honest.

'We should call Katrina,' Charlie added, nodding at Simon.

But before she could, her phone started ringing, echoing off of the attic beams. She rose to her feet, and pulling the phone from her coat pocket, she walked away to answer it.

'This isn't fair,' I said, barely whispering. My lips trembled even more ferociously and my eyebrows knitted as I began to sob.

Simon's grip on my shoulder tightened. I leaned into him. I knew that if anyone understood what I was feeling, it was him.

I hadn't known my parents. My memories of them were a collage of photos, stories, and possessions they left behind. My memories of them belonged to other people. I hadn't got to create any of my own memories with them. It wasn't fair.

But I know my sisters. I know Imogene.

I don't want her to turn into a memory.

I sobbed harder. For the first time in a long while, as I cried into Simon's shoulder, the shock threatening to drown me, I felt my age.

'I'm sorry I ran off,' I whimpered, wiping my eyes with the back of my hand.

Jerry licked my other hand. I patted him on the head, cherishing the feeling of his warm fur.

'It's my fault, isn't it,' I said, even quieter as the realisation dawned on me.

Simon spun me around, so that I was looking up at him, our faces almost mirroring each other.

'No,' he said, so firmly that if I didn't know him I would have thought he was furious. 'No, it isn't.'

I stared at him, before nodding silently.

'I need to see my sisters,' I whispered, straightening my shoulders and raising my head.

Charlie walked back over to us, the phone still held out in her hand. 'That was Abbey,' she said, pausing. 'They were checking the park. They – they think they found the car, the one that hit Imogene.'

In my state of shock I hadn't even contemplated who was responsible. Someone was responsible.

'Did they find the driver? How do they know it's the right car?' Simon asked.

Charlie pushed her hair back, the light from the skylights hitting her pale face severely. 'They found a red Volvo in the parking area of the park. The windshield is smashed in… and there's a lot of blood.' Her eyes flew hesitantly to me as she added this detail.

A *red* car. A thought was banging at the door at the back of my mind, but I couldn't quite reach the doorknob.

'They said they are going to have a look around the park before calling the police.'

Imogene had been hit. There was no one who wanted to hurt Imogene more than the ghostly figure banging at the back of my mind.

'We need to go to the park,' I said, standing up and pushing the blanket off me. Jerry stood up too, as his rest was disturbed, and he padded off out of the room.

Charlie looked uneasily at Simon. 'I think we should take you to the hospital,' she said slowly.

'I'm going to the park. I'll help Leo and Abbey look. I'm going to help!' My voice rose loudly as I began walking quickly towards the door.

Simon grabbed my arm and pulled me to a sudden halt. He looked down at me, his stony face reading mine like an open book.

'Don't. Ever. Run off again,' he said quietly, each word bearing down on me. He let go of my arm. 'We'll call Katrina and tell her we found you, that you're safe, and that we're going to the hospital,' he said, looking between Charlie and I authoritatively.

'But first we'll go to the park, and see if there's anything worth reporting to the police.' He said this last part looking only at me.

He'd never felt more like a brother to me than he did in that moment.

I grabbed a raincoat from the banister and together the three of us walked to Simon's car. Charlie got in the back seat so that I could sit in the front.

The wind had calmed but the rain continued to fall with full force.

'Thank you,' I said, looking first at Simon and then craning my neck back to look at Charlie.

I didn't know what had happened between Joanna and Charlie this summer, but I knew that if anything bad had happened between them, it meant nothing now that she was here.

I couldn't help but feel sheepish; my family was in the hospital and I had been hiding in an attic. Despite what Simon had said, I was responsible. I was responsible, but now I was going to help.

It took us less than ten minutes to get to the park. Charlie had called Katrina whilst we were driving, and had also let Abbey and Leo know we were coming so that they could meet us. Simon pulled into the park entrance and stopped in the car parking area. It was practically deserted.

I got out of the car as quickly as I could. Across the car park I saw Abbey and Leo. They got out of their car as we did. Abbey ran over to me and pulled me into a hug. She didn't say anything, but when she pulled away her face was a weary mixture of tear streaks and rain-soaked hair. It made me feel even worse. They had been looking for me when they could have been in the hospital. It was where I should have been.

Leo and Abbey led us over the grass to where they had found the car. The park was vast in comparison to the small square car-park.

The grass was torn up where it had been driven over, and the muddy tracks were clear. We followed the tracks. The car had been driven into a group of bushes, obviously brought to a stop only when the metal of the bonnet met the bark of a now twisted oak tree.

I started to run ahead, but slowed when I remembered Simon's warning. The cold night air caught in my throat like a steel knife lodged horizontally. The rain chilled my face, but my blood felt like burning metal.

The others walked up behind me. Simon surveyed the blood-splattered windshield. Abbey hid her eyes. Leo swore bloody murder, certain it had to be the car. Simon's eyes could not be torn away, his face a mask of rage.

My eyes remained transfixed by the very thing I had thought I'd see. The door in the back of my mind had been flung wide open, and my consciousness was screaming.

I couldn't take my eyes off the dent. In the passenger door of the beaten and bloody red Volvo that lay before me, a dent was carved into the weapon of my sister's pain, like an 'x' on a map.

TWENTY TWO

Simon

Despite the efforts of the rain to wash the car clean, this portrait of destruction remained fairly intact. The surrounding foliage did a lot to protect us where we stood next to the car, as the trees and bushes spread above us, providing shelter. However, the blood that was splattered across the front of the car did not entirely escape the falling water; where the raindrops landed, a crimson tear was formed.

I walked from the front of the car around to the passenger door where Jason stood, transfixed. Peering into the car I saw blood pooled in the driver's seat. I walked around to inspect it further.

The driver's door was swinging open, pushed back and forth by the wind. There was a dusting of glass over the inside of the car and the whole interior looked damp. My eyes were drawn up from the stale pool of blood on the seat to the crimson stamp on the headrest, dripping slowly down the chair.

'The driver must have been badly injured,' Abbey called over the sound of the wind. 'He probably lost control of the car, and tried to run on foot.'

'By the looks of it he can't have gone far.'

I backed away from the door. I looked over the car and Jason was still standing where I had left him. Sighing, I walked over to stand next to him.

His eyes remained fixed. 'It was Theo. This is Theo's car.'

'What?'

His eyes broke away to look up at me. Abbey and Leo walked over to us.

'What did you say?' Leo barked over the whistling of the wind.

'I recognise this car. The dent,' he said, pointing to the object of his fascination. 'This is definitely his car.'

It was undeniable; it made sense.

'He did it on purpose,' Jason said, louder this time. His face twitched as anger threatened to take control of him. His hands were balled into fists at his sides.

Abbey was a voice of reason after the pause that followed Jason's accusation. 'We should call the police.' She reached to get her phone from her pocket.

I turned to look around us. With the amount of blood in the car he definitely couldn't have got far.

Jason shared the same thought. 'He could still be here,' he said fervently. 'He's probably still here!'

'We don't know it's him, Jason,' Abbey said quietly, lowering the phone from her ear.

'He's right,' Charlie whispered. 'This is his car.'

We all exchanged tormented looks.

'Then the police will find him,' Leo said resolutely. 'Go ahead, Abbey.'

'But...' Jason began.

'Jason, they'll find him,' Charlie nodded conciliatorily.

But this wasn't enough to pacify him. He turned frantically in a circle, his eyes searching every part of the park they could reach.

I went to put my hand on his shoulder but he shoved me away, and bolted around the car, further into the park.

'Call the police!' I shouted at Abbey backing away before turning to run.

It didn't matter that I was taller and faster than Jason; he was determined. When I caught up with him he simply shouted at me, frantically turning his head this way and that, searching.

'I'm not running away again! I just want to find him!'

'Jason, will you stop!'

He was desperate. I could tell he just wanted to do something to help; anything but sit in a hospital waiting for bad news.

The occasional street lamp flickered here and there, but they were so sparsely placed throughout the park that it felt as if we were running with our eyes closed. If the light had been better we might have been able to see footprints in the muddy grass, or spot blood that had dripped to the ground from the driver – from Theo. Instead, it was all I could do to watch out for Jason beside me.

He ignored the paths, and ran instead along the grass, as the driver had obviously veered to hide the car. If he was here he would be trying his best not to be found.

Jason pulled up short. I had to put both my hands down on his shoulders to stop myself barrelling him over.

'I... I thought I heard something,' he said quietly, breathing heavily.

I stopped. I listened.

A few metres to the right of us it sounded as if someone was moaning. A street light down the path provided a bit of illumination.

I knew where we were. To our right, a row of bushes hid a narrow wall that marked where a bike shed used to be.

Jason stepped forward. I grabbed his arm. I gave him a stern look, and he must have understood because he moved back so that his body was behind mine.

I turned my head around to look behind us, but I couldn't see Leo and Abbey.

Turning back to Jason I bent down slightly so that I was looking him clearly in the eye. 'You stay close to me, and you do *exactly* as I say.'

He nodded, but his chest rose and fell fiercely.

I straightened up, and taking a deep breath I moved forward.

The sounds were undeniable now. Someone was moaning, crying out in pain. We were a couple of feet away from the wall when the hidden figure among the bushes cursed loudly.

The street lamp threw our shadows diagonally. I pushed a stray branch away from my path and something caught my eye on the ground below.

My stomach turned, and I grunted in disgust. There was blood all over the ground.

'Is that…'

I pushed Jason back behind me as I walked around the bushes, following the path of blood. He pushed back against my arm.

It was Theo; it was his blood. He was slumped against the wall, gripping his blood-soaked abdomen, hitting his head repeatedly back against the bricks.

He looked up from the ground, frantically searching our faces. He opened his mouth to talk, but only a gurgled scream escaped. His teeth dripped with a mixture of saliva and blood. He spat onto the floor, but the excess dribbled down his chin.

I took my phone from my pocket and dialled quickly, relishing the seconds I didn't have to look at the shattered human in front of me.

A mechanical-sounding woman answered the call.

'I need an ambulance.' I spoke quickly, but my heavy breathing threatened to suffocate the words from me.

'What are you doing?' Jason shouted. He reached up, hitting my arm with all his force.

The phone flew out of my un-expecting grasp, clattering across the ground.

I looked at him, my mouth hanging open with shock. 'Jason, he needs an ambulance! He's dying.'

I shoved him back, causing him to stumble, as I searched the ground for my phone.

But he darted in front of me. He put both of his palms on my chest and shoved. I hit his hands out of the way with ease.

'Jason!'

He recoiled from my voice, but stood his ground.

'Why does he deserve our help?' he said quietly, an anger flooding his voice that I had never thought him capable of.

'What?' I shook my head despairingly. I couldn't understand.

Just then Charlie burst around the corner, skidding to a halt when her eyes found us. Then they found Theo.

She gasped and her hands shot up to her face, covering her mouth, her eyes widening as they took in his mangled state. She looked back and forth between where Jason and I stood in apparent confrontation, and where Theo stayed slumped against the wall. She went over to him and threw off her coat. Her nose pinched in disgust, she placed her coat on his abdomen where the blood seemed to be most ferociously gushing. I noticed the piece of glass protruding from him.

'The police are on their way. Abbey and Leo stayed at the car park to meet them.'

She shook her head, as anger and sadness sought to tear her expression in two.

'Why the fuck did you do it?' she whispered.

Theo laughed. He actually *laughed*. His face grew ten times more menacing as his blood-soaked mouth took centre stage on his face.

But he didn't answer.

He didn't look at Charlie. He looked at me. I looked back at him.

His eyes already looked dead.

'Why are you helping him?' Jason shouted, tears streaming down his pale face. He threw his arms up in exasperation, as he moved towards his foe.

Charlie surveyed Jason in bewilderment. 'He...' She shook her head. 'Stopping him from bleeding to death won't stop him from paying for what he did, Jason.'

Jason didn't move. He stood there, tears rolling down his cheeks, his eyes captured by Theo.

I knelt down next to Charlie to help. 'I tried to call an ambulance but... Can you use your phone?'

She shook her head, 'I left it in the car.'

Theo grabbed the front of my T-shirt. I felt his blood seep through the cotton to caress my skin.

I recoiled, grabbing his wrist and pinning his arm to the floor. My teeth were so tightly clamped together that I thought any minute they might shatter. I no longer felt the cold, only the anger burning throughout my body.

I knew I wouldn't, but part of me wanted to agree with Jason. Part of me asked, *Why should we help him?*

'He's the reason why my family's dying. He's the reason they're lying in hospital!' Jason suddenly screamed and ran forward.

Simultaneously, as Charlie shouted his name, warding him off with a bloody palm, I jumped up and grabbed him around the waist, pulling him back. He cried and screamed, and fought against me.

'Let him go. There isn't much of me left, but he's welcome to whatever of me is.' Theo spoke in harsh gurgled whispers, coughing after each sentence as if each sentence might be his last.

'Haven't you done enough damage?' Charlie spat back at

him, applying even more pressure to his wound as the blood persisted in escaping him.

'Why do you care?' Theo said, his voice surprisingly quiet. He sat back and watched the chaos unfolding around him. 'She was going to leave you. She doesn't care about anyone but herself.' He dismissed us.

With renewed ambition Jason fought to escape the iron grip with which I held him.

'You loved her, you evil son of a bitch. You loved her and she didn't love you back because she saw how black your soul really is. And you just couldn't stand how much she loved her family, because you know how much they love her also. You were jealous, and it was that *pathetic* jealousy which sat you behind that wheel,' Charlie said firmly, unwavering.

'You're wondering why we should help him, Jason?' she paused, shaking her head. 'We're helping him because we're nothing like him.'

Jason continued to sob, but his flailing limbs stilled.

'She's right, Jason. You know she is.'

My phone started ringing. I could spot it now, the screen illuminated where it lay a couple of metres away.

As I felt the tension easing from Jason, I carefully relaxed my grip. He was still sobbing, but the sobs no longer held a hysterical tone.

I remained where I stood as Jason walked over to Theo. He knelt next to him. He looked from the blood dripping down his face from a small cut on his head, to the seeping wound on which Charlie still applied pressure. Charlie watched him carefully.

Fresh tears pricked his eyes, but he closed his lips against the sobs that shook him. 'They're all I have left, and you tried to take them from me.'

Theo had started to shake erratically, and he had stopped banging his head against the wall. I think he had lost the energy to move at all. He was a prisoner in Jason's gaze.

Jason swallowed, and nodded his head earnestly, wiping the tears away from his eyes with the back of his hands. He turned to me. 'Call them.'

I ran over to where I had seen my phone illuminate. I clawed the floor until I found it, and dialled as soon as my fingers reached it. I told them where we were, I gave them all the details I could. I could already hear the sirens of the police approaching us.

Jason took off his coat, mimicking Charlie, and attempted to dab at Theo's comparatively minor wounds.

Theo hadn't stopped watching him. 'She's right,' he whispered, cut off by a cough that threatened to drain what little energy he had left.

Jason looked to Charlie and back at me, but we couldn't answer his questioning look.

'You are better than me,' Theo explained, closing his eyes. 'Just like she is.'

TWENTY THREE

Joanna

When I was little I was afraid of the dark. It was an irrational fear. Even then, I knew it was irrational. But just because I told myself I shouldn't be afraid, because other people told me I shouldn't be afraid, it didn't mean I wasn't, that I could simply not be afraid.

My parents used to close my bedroom door when they thought I was finally asleep. I would wake up and yell for them to leave it open so that the light from the landing would stream through the crack into my room.

I got over my fear of the dark, eventually. I would concentrate on other things. I would imagine stories like movies in my head. I would focus on the sound of the waves crashing onto the beach beyond our garden. I would grip fistfuls of my duvet in my hands and focus on how the material felt within my grasp. Eventually the fear just went away.

But this was a different kind of darkness.

I was strangely aware that I had just been awake. I can't explain it. I wasn't aware of time or space, but I somehow remembered that I was in hospital. Katrina was here. But the others weren't. I remembered that much. But I must have blacked out again before she explained why.

This darkness scared me because I was aware. It's like when you're dreaming, but you know you're dreaming. It's like being in a dark room, but there not being a light switch.

I held onto the sounds of the crashing waves. It was so peaceful. Images filled my mind, and I let them sweep across my eyes, caressing my subconscious. The waves, the sand dunes, and Jerry galloping through the shallow water. Figures moved up and down the coast, but their faces were blurred into obscurity.

I sighed. If this was what death was like then I didn't mind it.

But death had not chosen me; not yet.

'Wake up,' he whispered. His hand stroked my hair back from my face.

For once I wasn't sure I wanted to leave the darkness. It was ominously peaceful. The voice was showing me the way towards the light switch, but I wasn't sure I wanted to find it.

But the peacefulness was breaking. The crashing waves were replaced by screeching metal. There was a pain in my head. It had been there before; I recognised it.

I lurched myself towards the light switch.

'Hey. Hey there.'

I made some incomprehensible noise as I opened my eyes. My throat was dry. My eyes blinked hard against the lights glaring down at me from the ceiling. I turned my head away from the fluorescents and found the face of my best friend watching me.

'How nice of you to return to us,' he smiled, the skin around his deep brown eyes crinkling jovially.

His hair was abnormally messy, strands sticking out chaotically, and the shadows under his eyes aged him by ten years.

My blinking slowed as my eyes adjusted. I became aware of my breathing and sighed, relishing the air that rushed in and out of my lungs. I moved my head around, as my eyes took in my surroundings. I tried to push myself up onto my elbows, and succeeded with more exertion that it should have taken.

I had been right; I was in a small hospital room. The space where Katrina had hovered was now empty, but the rest was there. My bed was in the centre of the room. A generic pastoral painting hung above two armchairs opposite my bed. There was no window, but an air conditioning grille overhead provided a cold draft. The door was to my left behind Simon, who was sitting on a tall chair, leaning over the side of my bed, watching me vigilantly.

'There's blood on your T-shirt,' I whispered, my voice croaky. I reached out and felt the front of his shirt, feeling the dried, crimson stain.

Memories fought their way to the forefront.

'The others…' My hand gripped the front of his T-shirt, as I panicked. My eyes searched the room for bodies that I knew were not there. 'The car…' my voice drifted off as I fell back onto the pillow behind me. My hand went up to caress my throbbing head.

'Calm down,' Simon said, standing up as he frowned down at me. His appearance did nothing to calm me.

I remembered. 'There was a car… it hit me. Where's Jason?' My panic received fresh fervour as I remembered my little brother's figure disappearing into the night.

'He's OK. He's in the hall.' Simon took my hand in his, and laid his other hand on my forearm, caressing my scars with his thumb. I slowed my breathing, but panic still ate away at my insides.

I nodded up at him. *My brother's OK*, I repeated inside my head.

'Joanna,' he said slowly, sitting down on the side of my bed instead of back in his chair. I didn't take my eyes away from his. He was so hard to read. 'You weren't hit by the car.'

I instinctively shook my head. The pain normalised

to a rhythmic throbbing in the back of my head. 'I don't understand. I remember the car.'

'There was a car,' he nodded. His frown deepened. 'It was going to hit you, but Imogene pushed you out of the way. You were knocked unconscious when you hit the floor. You lost a lot of blood and the crack in your skull was pretty bad, I think.'

I closed my eyes. I felt dizzy. It felt as if I was suddenly swimming in the open air. I had remembered the car coming towards me, but I hadn't remembered her pushing me out of the way. But I did now. As if summoned by Simon's words, I felt the ghost of Imogene's hands push against me.

My head pounded even harder.

She had been hit. She had let herself be hit, so I wouldn't be.

My eyes shot open. 'Where is she? Is she OK?' I was almost shouting at him, clinging on to him as I squeezed his hand tightly.

His eyes bore into mine. He seemed to weigh each word carefully as he spoke, reading every inch of my face as he assessed how much he thought I could take.

'They said she's going to be OK. She lost a lot of blood, Jo. Her injuries are bad.' His eyes fell from mine for the first time, choosing the sight of our intertwined hands instead. 'She's going to be in here for a while. And... and her scarring is pretty bad. They had to remove a lot of glass from her face and arms.'

Cold tears seemed to burn against the warmth of my flushed cheeks. 'But she's alive? She's going to be OK?' I began to weep.

He let go of my hand and pulled me into him, wrapping his arms tightly around me. 'She going to be OK, Jo. It's OK.'

She was scarred, she had bled, but she was still here.

'Who did it?' I asked, my face still buried in his shoulder. 'Did they find the driver?'

I heard him sigh, his chest rising and falling dramatically against me. 'Theo was driving. We found him in the park. He had crashed his car into a tree. His injuries were really bad when we found him. The paramedics said they thought he was under the influence.'

I pulled back from him.

'Theo.' I repeated it quietly to myself. It was weird to be so completely taken aback by something, and yet completely unsurprised.

'Jo.' He put his hand under my chin to bring my eyes back to his. 'Theo died.'

I let his hand hold the weight of my head. My mouth moved, but I couldn't find any words.

I didn't want this. I had never wanted *this*.

'You found him?'

He nodded. 'Abbey and Leo found the car in the park. Jason, Charlie and I found him further in. He had tried to run on foot after crashing the car the second time.'

My eyes dropped, and returned to his blood-stained shirt. 'That's his blood.' I nodded; it wasn't a question. We lapsed into silence.

'What are you thinking?' Simon asked eventually.

I looked around the room, at the painting hanging over the armchairs. I could hear voices in the hall. I didn't want to think. I was tired of feeling angry, of feeling scared, and sorrowful. I didn't want to pity Theo, but I did. I was sorry he was dead, and that made me feel something I had no idea how to explain to my best friend as he watched me nervously.

So I sighed, expelling my unwanted thoughts. 'I was thinking that I want to see the others now.' I gently pushed his guarding hands away from me, and swung my legs over the side of the bed. I felt something tug in my arm at my sudden movement, and realised that I was connected to a machine. My head swam and the pounding grew.

'No, no, no,' Simon repeated, stopping me from moving any further as he placed his hands on my shoulders. I gave in and fell back onto the bed. For the first time since being awake, I saw him smile. 'I'll bring them to you,' he chuckled.

He got up and walked towards the door. He paused briefly with his back towards me before reaching for the handle and disappearing into the hallway.

Jason burst into the room less than a minute later. He barely paused at the door before hurling himself onto the bed and wrapping his arms around me. I was in pain, but that didn't stop me from hugging him back. The others followed him: Katrina, Abbey, Leo, Charlie. Even Mrs Vincent and Simon's mum came in shortly after.

It felt as if I still wasn't quite awake. Jason told me everything that had happened, saying over and over again how stupid he was to have run, but how he would never leave again. He also had traces of blood on his clothes, the very sight of which unnerved me. Abbey cried, and eventually gave up repeatedly wiping her glasses and took them off, putting them into her pocket. Katrina explained to me exactly what was going on, what the doctors had said. Her hair was even wilder than usual. She spoke so maturely, as if her soul had finally caught up with her real age.

I wasn't aware of the time ticking by as we sat in the hospital room. My fingernails had begun to dig anxiously into my palm by the time Simon's mum offered to ferry people home. Mrs Vincent was going to take Jason home to get him some fresh clothes and dinner, before bringing him back later. Katrina and Simon were the only ones left, then Katrina said that she was going to get a drink from the vending machine down the hallway.

'You're not going with your mum?' I asked Simon.

'She's going to give Jason a change of clothes for me, to bring back with him,' was all Simon replied. 'Are you trying to get rid of me?' he mocked, raising his eyebrows at me.

I smiled back, closing my eyes as I leaned back on the pillow.

I didn't ward off the darkness as tiredness hit me; I welcomed it. I let my body relax into the thin mattress of the hospital bed. I welcomed the sound of the waves.

I dreamed of the accident, but this time it was different. There was no screaming; there was no crying; the flames were there, but I did not feel them as they licked at my arm. Instead of the pain, my focus was on the faces.

It was as if I was watching a film that I had already seen. It was like reading a book but with the emotional detachment of already knowing how the story ends. I remembered everything now. Nine years later, and I remembered everything.

I saw my mum's face as she looked back at us for the last time. I saw my own ten-year-old face, screwed up with the effort of pulling my siblings from the wreckage. I saw my sacrifice, and I saw Imogene's face as she realised how this day would haunt her.

I saw her face nine years later; I saw the determination in her eyes as she pushed me from death's path. I saw her sacrifice.

I saw Theo, and I saw his anger. I saw beyond the hands on the wheel, to the pain that ate away at him behind his eyes.

I saw Jason's face as the rain hit his eyes. I saw his tears as he thought his worst fear had come true, and I saw his smile as he jumped upon my bed; today was not the day.

I saw the strength in Katrina's face as she made her brother proud. I saw Mrs Vincent and the story each wrinkle told. I saw Allana and the weight of Simon's father's departure upon her shoulders. I saw the resolve which kept her head held high.

Then I saw Simon's face, and the waves crashed harder as they formed the orchestra of my dream. I saw Leo and Abbey and Charlie. I saw them all, and I didn't want to dream any more.

I wanted to live.

When I woke, I was relieved to find my arm no longer attached to the machine beside my bed. Simon lay slumped across the armchairs, fast asleep. Slowly, making each step as if I were learning to walk for the first time, I walked across to him. I shook him awake. His eyes were wide, startled, as he lurched awake. He surveyed me frantically, looking back at the bed I had just climbed out of.

'What's wrong?'

'Nothing,' I assured him, as he frowned. 'I want to see her.'

TWENTY FOUR

Imogene

I didn't look like them. Their auburn hair contrasted with my blonde like autumn leaves against the summer sun. My piercing blue eyes were like the sky, and their hazel eyes like the forest below.

But I was like them. I *am* like them. I didn't share their blood. I didn't share their looks. I shared their story.

I was staring at the cream-coloured ceiling, my eyes blurred as I focused on nothing in particular. I didn't move because my body ached relentlessly. I didn't speak because I wasn't sure I could make the words come out.

I let my thoughts swim around my consciousness instead. I let myself think, actually think about everything that had happened, about all the shit that had been banging against the door at the back of my mind for all this time. The door was open, and my thoughts were galloping free.

My parents had never played any instruments. My dad had been tone-deaf, to say the least. I thought I had at least shared their lack of musical talent. I had been wrong. Our biggest discrepancy turned out to be the source of my greatest talent.

I could hear the music now. Lying on my hospital bed staring at the ceiling, I could hear the sorrowful elegance of an instrument that had both proved my worth and cemented my greatest fear in my mind. Life was full of little ironies like that.

I realised I was crying only as the tear dropped off the tip of my chin. My heart hurt with an intensity that was more crippling than the power of any car. I closed my eyes and let the tears flow freely down my cheeks.

'I miss you.'

I said it aloud. For the first time in nine years I said it aloud.

The music swept over me and I breathed in each note that hit me. Thoughts swirled through my mind as if orchestrated to perform the most intricate of dances. I let them. I opened my mind and I welcomed the music.

I had been so stupid. I smiled, blinking another tear from my eye. I was so tired. I had been fighting for the fight's own sake. It doesn't get much more stupid than that.

I opened my eyes, and sighed. I looked down at my crippled body. There was a needle going into my left arm, connecting me to a machine beeping monotonously by the side of my bed. There was what looked like, a padded plaster covering most of my right arm, and I could feel something similar pressing down on my upper abdomen. My head thumped slowly, in time with my blinking as I surveyed myself. There were some scratches along my left forearm. I reached up to touch my head and I felt stitching above my left eyebrow. There was a plaster covering the lower bit of my left cheek and most of my neck. I could feel the skin sinking tiredly below my eyes, and as I brought my hand in front of my face I saw how thin and bruised my hand looked.

I couldn't help but laugh to myself. *I must look like Frankenstein*, I thought to myself.

There was a knock at the door.

The door opened timidly, and Jason's head appeared through it. He was about half the height of the door frame, so I could barely see him over the foot of bed.

I cleared my throat. 'It's about time you came to see me.' My voice still came out croaky, but I smiled nonetheless.

He laughed shyly, walking slowly into the room. 'They finally said we could come in and see you,' he said, pointing with his thumb back towards the door. He stopped by my bed, resting his hands on the covers, nervously fiddling with a loose thread. 'How are you feeling?'

'Awful,' I laughed, raising my beaten arm as evidence.

'You do look pretty awful,' he nodded, before smiling. He pointed to my face. 'Does it hurt?'

'Everything hurts right now,' I sighed. 'But it's nothing I can't handle.'

He climbed up onto the side of my bed, crossing his legs under himself, his posture straight and his head held high as he frowned at me, looking at each of my injuries individually.

'Tell me,' I said, after a minute or so of silence passed us by. 'Fill me in on everything.'

He did; he told me everything. He told it factually, relaying events with the seeming maturity of an adult delivering the news. However, as the story unfolded I could tell he was putting it on, I guessed for my sake. Relief doesn't begin to describe how I felt when he told me Joanna was OK. But when he described finding Theo, I saw the toll that everything had taken on him. He lowered his eyes to the bed and fiddled excessively with the sheet. I closed my eyes and rested my head back on the stacked pillows behind me as he told me the rest.

Theo was dead. He had died trying to kill me, by almost killing Joanna.

It was only at that part of the story that I began to cry again. I kept my eyes closed as my chin quivered and my shoulders shook. Jason took my hand in his.

Had he hated me that much? Why else would he have done it?

I wiped my eyes and pushed myself tentatively into a sitting position. Jason watched me carefully, not letting go of my hand.

'Where are the others?'

As if summoned by my question Joanna burst through the door, throwing it back against the wall. Her eyes were big and round as she looked from me to Jason, and then looked me up and down. She panted heavily.

'I was getting coffee. They just told me you were... I only left for a second... I've been here every day since they let me go.'

'It's not like I'm going anywhere,' I joked, indicating my bed-bound body.

She walked forward to the other side of the bed from where Jason was sitting. She watched me even more nervously than Jason had when he walked in.

'I don't know what you're looking at me like that for. By the sounds of it you're the one with the busted-up head.'

She started laughing, but quickly dissolved into tears. Smiling as her eyes flooded, she threw herself towards me, wrapping her arms gently around my shoulders.

'It's like being in a parallel universe,' Jason said mockingly as he watched us hug. Joanna shoved him in the shoulder before pulling him in to join.

She was more like me than I had thought.

The nurse didn't let them stay for long, just long enough for Katrina to join us. I told them to go home; they all looked like they needed sleep. I told them to come back tomorrow. I didn't want them to leave, but my drooping eyelids disagreed.

I had to stay in the hospital for a few more days. Apparently I had lost a lot of blood, and also had internal bleeding. They tried to dumb it down so I would understand it; I was beaten up and would take a while to heal, but besides that I'd be fine. That's if you don't count the scarring.

It was the morning of the second day since I had woken up. I no longer felt as fragile, and so had asked the nurse for a mirror. I sat with one leg swinging over the side of the bed, facing the window on the outer wall of the room. The view wasn't dazzling; my room looked out onto a car park, roads and tall buildings. Nonetheless, I liked the light.

I held the mirror up to my face.

'Bloody hell,' I whispered, before snorting with laughter. Not a normal reaction to your own reflection. But I couldn't help it; I looked like an extra from a *Final Destination* film.

The cut above my eyebrow had been stitched neatly, and a few minor cuts and healing bruises decorated my face, but it was my left cheek and neck that stole the limelight. The nurse said I could leave the dressing off now, so the damage was revealed in all its glory. Moving down my left cheek and onto my neck was the mangled redness of healing skin. You could tell where bits of glass had directly hit the skin as the ghosts of smaller cuts dotted the greater canvas. The nurse warned me that it would scar noticeably. I moved the mirror around as I tried to look at it all from different angles. I settled on my eyes. Besides the bags, which weren't as bad as I had thought, my eyes were unchanged.

'At least it will be a conversation starter.'

I jumped, looking up abruptly to find Charlie standing in front of the open door. She was wearing a long black cardigan, over a white top, and black skinny jeans. Her jet black hair was tied back into a loose pony-tail. She held her hands together in front of her, moving back and forth on the balls of her feet. I wondered how long she had been standing there.

I put the mirror down on the bedside table. 'Because that's what you want your face to be – a conversation starter,' I laughed sarcastically, crossing my legs on the bed.

She laughed in a whispery kind of way, nervously. 'I'm sorry, that was a stupid thing to say.'

She walked forward slowly to the foot of my bed, leaning

on the rail. She looked back up at me, smiling kindly. 'You look well, though, all things considered. I was driving by, so I thought I'd just pop by to see how you were.'

I nodded curtly, and another moment of awkward silence ensued. 'I'm better, thank you. I can finally bear sitting up without wanting to throw up,' I said drolly.

She visibly relaxed momentarily, before her lips clamped shut over her smile. She brushed a non-existent piece of hair behind her ear.

'You know you can sit down if you want,' I prompted, indicating to the uncomfortable-looking chairs around the room.

She stepped back, sitting down in an armchair near the foot of the bed, before abruptly standing back up again.

I had to resist the urge to laugh, summoning all of my patience.

'Thank you.' This really caught her off guard, and a smile broke free across my lips.

'For what?'

'They told me how you helped to find Jason, how you were there when they found Theo. Thank you.' I looked her in the eye when I spoke. I wanted her to realise how earnest I was being.

'I don't deserve it.' She looked down at her twiddling hands as a dull redness coloured her porcelain cheeks. She was breathing heavily through her nose as her mouth was clamped shut, tension in her jaw.

She sighed heavily, looking to the ceiling for answers. 'I was so *horrible* to you,' she accentuated each word heavily. 'I... I thought you deserved it. I helped Theo... those things I said... You didn't deserve any of it.' Her mouth clamped shut again, and she blinked hard to keep the tears from shedding. 'I'm so sorry, and I know that is the least I can say, but I really do mean it,' she rushed, searching my eyes intensely for acceptance.

'I don't know if Joanna told you, but I've been going through some stuff,' she continued, shaking her head.

'She didn't have to tell me,' I said bluntly. She stared at me frowning, so I sighed and continued. 'It's easy enough for one broken bird to recognise another,' I said, pushing my hair back from my face.

Her shoulders dropped, relaxing. She walked over and sat in a chair next to the head of my bed.

'I guess you and I are more alike than I would have ever admitted.'

'I think so too.'

In that moment I saw everything I had never opened my eyes to before. I saw a girl crying out; I saw a manifestation of my own reflection.

'When do you go back to university?'

'I'm not sure I'm going back,' she said, smiling sadly as she leaned back in the chair.

I leaned back on my stack of pillows. 'Well, if it makes you feel any better, I'm not sure what my next step is either.'

'I'm sorry to hear you didn't get the New York gig,' she said consolingly. 'Do you still have your job at the studio?'

'I think so. Katrina called them yesterday to explain, and they were understanding. And I guess I still have the orchestra.' I sighed.

'That doesn't sound convincing,' she grinned back, raising her eyebrows.

I shrugged. 'I'm not sure I want to go back either.'

'Are you still going to play?'

I frowned at her mockingly. 'Well, I'm definitely not going to do anything else. Will you transfer to a uni at home?' I asked her, curious.

She shook her again in confusion, laughing. 'I have no idea.'

'I don't suppose you've spoken to your parents about it?'

Her smile slipped away so quickly at the mention of her

parents. She shook her head. 'They're home tomorrow. I think it's time we had a chat.'

She raised her head to look at me. She wasn't smiling and she wasn't happy, but there was something so much more striking in her expression; she looked brave. Her head was raised, and her gaze unflinching, as if in that very moment she decided to take control of the reins. It was something I think I will always find hard to explain. It was a look I respected.

'Do you know, you're not as much of a bitch as I thought you were,' I said slyly.

She grinned, looking away at the window behind me, before looking back. 'You're not as crazy as I thought you were.'

'Oh I doubt that,' I countered. 'I think you'd definitely lose your mind trying to understand mine.'

So we made a deal; to never try to understand each other again.

I was discharged from the hospital three days later. I got in touch with my counsellor the next day. It didn't take long for the bricks upon my shoulders to build back up. But this time it was different; I was different. They put me on medication to help with the depression, and I took it. They asked me how I was, and I didn't just say 'OK'.

I was still fragile and so I was pretty much house-bound. Mary came to visit me, bringing me pieces that they were working on in the orchestra. I wrote new music and spent hours perfecting new pieces. I hung out with Jason when he came home from school, and with Katrina when she wasn't at work. Joanna recovered, physically, pretty quickly. She went back to her part-time job, and dividing her time between everyone before she went back to uni at the end of the month.

I didn't know how much she wanted to go back. I think part of her revelled in the idea of getting away for a bit, of focusing on something as straightforward as studying. But after everything that had happened, there was obviously a part of her that wanted to stay at home indefinitely. I still hadn't figured out my next step, but it was clear as day that Joanna's involved keeping hold of at least this part of normality.

It felt as if we had lived an entire lifetime in a single summer.

I was down on the beach when Simon came to talk to me. I was sitting in the same spot I had been in when Mrs Vincent had given me the letter of rejection.

He sat down next to me without saying a word.

I hadn't really spoken to him after everything, at least not alone. He had been at the house nearly every day over the past week, but so had Charlie and the others.

'Wow, calm down, Simon, don't talk my ear off,' I said drolly, after a couple minutes of silence passed us by.

He chuckled dryly, a smile breaking up his stony features. I picked up a pebble and threw it at the blue-green canvas in front of us. I turned to look at him, and he was looking at the water curiously.

'Did you know that Abbey and Leo are official now?'

I snickered, and mocked intrigue. 'Fascinating.'

He leant back on his elbows in bemusement. 'I know, right. I don't know how they're going to cope long-distance, though. But only time will tell,' he shrugged.

'Is that what you came to tell me? You disturbed me to inform me of your friends' relationship gossip?'

'I came to ask you how you are. But I thought I'd lighten the mood first; you know, pave the way for a deep conversation.'

'You're an idiot,' I laughed, shaking my head.

The wind was picking up, throwing the waves against each other before they reached the peace of the beach sand.

'I'm good. I'm better,' I said, thinking carefully before I answered.

He nodded pensively, sighing as he closed his eyes, letting the wind blow against his face.

'This is going to take a while to get used to, I think,' I said, turning my head to show him the now healed scars. 'But I don't mind it.'

'Did you know that Joanna has a tattoo?' he said all of a sudden.

I nodded. She had shown it to me before I had left the hospital. She had got it on the opposite arm to her scars. It was a sentence in Latin, written along her forearm. She didn't tell us what it meant. I could always take a picture and Google it, but that defeated the purpose. It was something for her. She said she had been thinking about it for a while; she had been playing with the idea that a scar wasn't so different to a tattoo. Both told a story. The scars on her arm were a story inflicted upon her, but the tattoo told one of her own choosing.

I didn't know how long I could fight my curiosity, and by the sounds of it curiosity was eating away at Simon as well.

'I just had no idea she was the tattoo type,' he rambled on.

I shrugged, and we sat in silence for a couple of minutes more. It's incredible how you can have an entire conversation without even uttering a word. The waves flowed, the seagulls hovered, and the pebbled sand crunched beneath me. I closed my eyes, breathing deeply.

'Maybe I should get a tattoo,' Simon pondered aloud.

My eyes remained closed, but my smile stretched across my face.

EPILOGUE

Joanna, One Year Later

Every time I returned home, something about the house was different. Ever since Imogene moved out, Katrina had viewed the entire house as a blank canvas, her creative spirit exploding forth with unrestrained force. She painted most of the rooms in the house, carefully characterising the decor of each room. The attic was unrecognisable; that had been Jason's idea. Instead of a room cluttered with stuff destined for the charity shops, or belongings the owners didn't care to ever see again, it was now a library.

The walls were newly insulated, sandpapered and painted, and the floorboards varnished. It was very much like the Vincents' library room, but with Jason and Katrina's own personal edge. Tall, light-oak bookshelves lined the three outer walls, but on the fourth wall hung photos, hundreds of them, plastered over every inch of the paint. Jason made us each chose our favourites and he had been adding to the collection over the past six months. Opposite this wall sat two white fabric-covered armchairs, each placed in a corner, facing a small coffee table that separated them.

On one bookshelf near the right armchair was his favourite photo, in a pale blue frame; it was a photo of himself, Mrs Vincent and Mr Vincent. It was on the bookshelf with all of the books they had given him. It was the bookshelf with the least space left on it.

Even Imogene was forced into the task of redecoration. However, her task lay in an entirely different house. Two months after she got out of hospital she started discussing the idea of renting a house with her friend Mary. She thought it was about time she got her own place. Mary's friend was renting out a three-bedroom house in the centre of town, and they jumped at the opportunity. However, they needed to find another roommate to fill the tenancy.

At the same time that Imogene was discovering her next step, Charlie was making a leap of faith. Against her parent's wishes she dropped out of university. They were furious, and made it clear that they would have no role in supporting her if she dropped out. It was as if she had finished one chapter of her life, only to discover that the next page was completely blank. It took a lot of courage for Charlie to make that step, to make a change by leaving an environment that she knew wasn't good for her. Imogene was there for her every step of the way; and they had found their third tenant.

They moved into the new house in January. Charlie got her job back at Abbey's parents' restaurant, and applied to study nursing at a more local university in September.

If you had asked me a year beforehand if I had ever imagined Charlie and Imogene living together, and becoming so close, I could not have answered with a more definitive 'No'.

Imogene kept her job at the studio, and remained a member of the orchestra. However, now this was only a backdrop to her greater ambitions. She was working harder on her writing skills, travelling to attend seminars and meet people in the music industry, and applied for a ton of different projects and positions.

It was by no means easy for her, but she was making the

steps she knew she needed to take. I had been home about three times since starting my second year at uni, and every time I was home I saw a bit more light shining through the blackness that shrouded her. Every so often a part of her reverted back, glass got smashed, tears got shed, and her mind led her away. However, I had no doubt in my mind that she would fight to get back. I knew I would never fully understand, and I knew that hers are not my problems to fix, but I don't think I had ever learned as much about my sister as I had in the past year and a half. I don't think I had ever realised how brave she really is.

I had been home for two days. I was sitting in the garden on an old blanket I had taken from the airing cupboard. Jerry was at the bottom of the garden, lounging in the high rising sun, whilst I shielded my eyes with my hand laid across my face.

I sighed and lay down onto my back.

'You know, I'm quite offended,' a voice said, as I heard footsteps crunching across the dried grass.

I smiled, but remained where I lay, the sun warming my eyelids. I didn't have to look.

'I've been home for less than forty-eight hours and I've already offended you, Simon?'

'Exactly. You've been home for forty-eight hours and you haven't come to see me. I'm offended,' he said, sitting on the blanket next to me.

'You've been home for a week already. I should be offended you haven't come to see me sooner.'

I opened my eyes, shading them with the back of my hand. He was smiling at the sun. His hair had got longer since I'd seen him last.

'Are you happy to be back?' he asked, turning to me, squinting to see me.

I nodded, moving up into a sitting position. 'You?'

'Yeah, I guess. Won't be long before I'm bored though,' he said dryly.

I laughed at him, leaning back on my hands. I was wearing a three-quarter-sleeved top. The sun hit the scars on my left arm, but it was the black ink on my right arm that was most noticeable. The ink shimmered as if the words were newly printed.

'You know, it's only four weeks until we leave,' I announced. 'So at least you won't be bored for long.'

Simon and I were going to Rome. Abbey, Leo and Charlie were going to meet us out there a couple of days later as Charlie had to work until then, and Abbey and Leo were staying with Leo's grandparents in Edinburgh.

He sighed happily at the thought. It had been his suggestion. At first, it was just going to be the two of us, but then Leo got so excited at the idea that we made it a group thing. I didn't mind, but Simon took a bit more convincing. I was just content with the idea of travelling.

'How's Imogene?' he asked, abruptly.

'She's good, busy. I was round at her house yesterday, and she was showing me a new piece she's working on.'

It was only recently that she had started playing in front of us again. I relished every opportunity to hear her play, especially if it was something of her own creation.

'She's going to Berlin this summer, isn't she?'

'In about a month,' I nodded.

She was going with Mary, as they had both got internships over there. I thought back to when she had got the news. She had applied on a whim, it was just one of the many things she was trying for. But then she got it, and suddenly she wasn't so sure. She would be away for three weeks, during which a date which had caused so much chaos last year would reoccur, and with it the emotions that had threatened to break her.

I told her to take it.

Every year, for far too long, I had tried to enforce what I considered appropriate remembrance upon those who also felt the loss of my mum and dad. It would be the tenth anniversary of their death this year. So I told her she should go. Remembering someone shouldn't revolve around a date, it shouldn't be highlighted through ceremony. What better way to remember them, than going to Berlin and doing what made her happy, what made her proud? What better way to remember them, than through what she was doing with her life ten years after their deaths?

It had felt like an epiphany; a very long overdue one at that. We would struggle, we would cry and we would get sad. People we loved had died, and that would never be OK. I wanted to fix it and I couldn't. All I could do was try to make the ride a bit smoother.

I thought of the idea of your life being a story, and that made it easier to explain. Their books were closed, but their stories weren't over. Their characters lived on in mine, in Jason's, Katrina's and Imogene's stories. We remembered them and we honoured them in every word. Our books weren't closed yet. At least, that's how I liked to think of it.

So she took the internship.

I was staring off into the distance, lost in a reverie, when Simon started playing with my hand. He was lying on his stomach next to me, tracing the inside of my palm idly with his fingers. His left eye was closed against the glare of the sun, but the deep brown of his other eye was revealed in between lazy blinks, watching his hand dance with mine.

'If I lie here much longer I might fall asleep. I didn't tell you I saw Marcus Grisham the other day.'

I didn't take my eyes off our dancing hands, but my heart strained momentarily, and my lips moved nervously against each other. Marcus Grisham was Theo's older brother. I had never met him before last year, neither had Imogene. Theo had spoken of him to her, but they were estranged. When I met him, I wasn't surprised. Marcus was married with a little boy. He was an accountant now, having left home as soon as he could by the sounds of it. We spoke to the police a lot after the hit and run, but didn't meet Marcus until a couple of weeks after. He approached us. He came by the house, and stayed for a coffee.

'Where did you see him?'

'Just in town. I saw him crossing the road. He didn't recognise me, I don't think.'

I had tried to read Marcus, tried to understand how he felt about Theo's death, about the way he had died. But he was unreadable. He didn't seem to know what to say. He must have felt some sense of guilt by association. He explained how he was Theo's next of kin, but that had become nothing but a legal thing: He hadn't seen his brother for years. He was a sombre kind of man. He relayed events to us as they had been explained to him by the police. He told us he was sorry for everything that had happened.

He had said this when he saw Imogene, her face a portrait of the events. I felt bad for him. He hadn't known his brother for years, and now this was all he would ever know of him. He never tried to justify his character, or to explain that he didn't know where it had all gone wrong, and he never displayed any animosity towards us for what had happened. He accepted it all.

'I wonder what he was doing back here?' I asked, sighing remorsefully.

Simon shrugged, shaking his head.

I wondered if I would ever see him again.

We sat in the garden for another couple of hours, talking of whatever floated into our heads. We didn't talk about Theo or Marcus, and that thread of thought drifted away from us. The lowering sun had immersed us in the shadow of late afternoon when Simon said he had to go. I walked through the house with him as I wanted to go by and see Mrs Vincent.

I noticed her sitting on her front step when we got to the end of my driveway. She waved at us, watching us from where she sat as her youthful smile lit up her face.

Simon waved back, laughing at her obvious watchfulness. 'I swear she'll outlive us all.'

We paused at the end of the driveway as we had to go in opposite directions. I smiled as I looked over my shoulder at her. She gave the illusion of surveying her garden, but nothing escaped her vigilant eyes. I turned back to Simon, and his eyes were on me.

'What?' I asked, suddenly very aware of myself.

'Nothing,' he said, looking away as he fought a smile. He began to back away. 'I'll see you tomorrow.'

'Wait, what's tomorrow?'

'We have plans,' he said, losing out to the smile as he turned to walk away.

'No, we don't,' I corrected him, now talking to his back.

'We do now,' he called over his shoulder, before striding down the road.

I pushed my hair behind my ear, shaking my head. I walked through the front gate, and into the floral haven of Mrs Vincent's front garden. I sat on the step next to her, leaning my forearms against my knees.

'I know what you're thinking,' I said, peering over at her, as she inspected a potted tree on the step next to her; at least, that's what she appeared to be doing.

'That's very presumptuous of you, Joanna,' she said slowly. I raised my eyebrows at her. 'It's his mother you should be worried about. I'm pretty sure she already has a wedding venue in mind for the two of you,' she said, offhandedly.

'How are you?' I asked, dragging out each word to emphasise the blunt change in topic.

'I can't complain.'

'How is Robert doing?'

She turned to look at me, and shook her head slowly, gently. He was deteriorating quickly.

'Is there anything I can do?'

She sighed and gazed past me, looking over her garden. A woman walked past the gate with a dog padding along beside her.

'This. This right here is what you can do.'

And so I did.

I sat with Mrs Vincent nearly every afternoon that summer, whenever I could. Jason came over to read with Mr Vincent as much as he could, especially once he got off school for the summer. Mr Vincent stopped recognising him after a while, but Jason kept going. The worse Mr Vincent got, the more determined Jason was to spend every minute he could with him.

I had taken Mrs Vincent to a garden centre the day Mr Vincent died, in late August. She had got a call from his nurse, and he passed away shortly after we got back to the house.

Even then she didn't complain.

'Simon would look very nice in a suit,' she continued to tease me, that day on the step.

I cupped my face in my hands in mock despair. And then nostalgia hit me, a page reprinted further along in the book. 'Have I ever asked you the thing about if your life was a book?'

She stared at me, intrigued.

'If you were given a book containing the events of your life, from birth to death, would you read it? Would you read it to the end?'

She smiled, clasping her hands together on her lap. 'You're forgetting who first asked you that one, my dear.'

'Of course! I forgot it was you who asked me,' I shook my

head, as the memory of the first time she had asked me flowed back into my mind. 'Well, then, would you?'

She paused, frowning as she considered the question, before answering bluntly, 'No.'

She never explained why.